# STEP BROTHER

*with Benefits*

## SECOND SEASON

# MIA CLARK

# DEDICATION

Thank you to Ethan and Cerys for helping me with
this book and everything involved in the process.
This is a dream come true and I wouldn't have been
able to do it without them. Thank you, thank you!

# CONTENTS

# ACKNOWLEDGMENTS

Thank you for taking a chance on my book!

I know that the stepbrother theme can be a difficult one to deal with for a lot of people for a variety of reasons, and so I took that into consideration when I was writing this. While this is a story about forbidden love, it's also a story about two people becoming friends, too. Sometimes you need someone to push you in your life, even when you think everything is fine. Sometimes you need someone to be there, even when you don't know how to ask them to stay with you.

This is that kind of story. It is about two people becoming friends, and then becoming lovers. The forbidden aspects add tension, but it's more than that, too. Sometimes opposites attract in the best way possible. I hope you enjoy my books!

# STEPBROTHER WITH BENEFITS

## 1 - *Ashley*

THIS IS AWKWARD.

I guess I never truly realized how awkward this would be, but it's awkward. Going to dinner with my mom and Ethan's dad, with Ethan and me, is reminiscent of a double date. Do you know how awkward it is to be on a double date with your mom and stepdad? Um... well, if you don't you're about to find out.

We all drove here together. It seemed like a good idea to go to this restaurant we used to go to.

I don't know if we've all been here together before now, though. If I had to guess, I'd say we haven't, because as soon as we step inside, I remember how small the booths are.

"Four?" the hostess asks us.

Ethan's dad smiles and nods. "Yeah, just us."

"Alright," she says, smiling. "Right this way."

We follow her and she leads us to a corner booth. Which, um... yes. It's small. I think the corner ones are actually a little bigger than the others, but it's going to be a tight fit either way.

My mom sits down on the bench at one side of the table and Ethan's dad sits down next to her. Yes, I suppose I should mention that they always sit next to each other, which means...

Ethan and I stare at each other, not sure what to do. The hostess keeps looking at us funny, too. Ethan's dad is kind of oblivious, and I'm not sure if my mom has realized the predicament we're in right now.

"Is something the matter?" the hostess asks us.

"Nah," Ethan says with a shrug. To me, he adds, "Sorry, Princess. Looks like it's you and me together."

Yeah, well, you know what, Ethan? I like that! Um... I usually would like that, except I'm supposed to pretend I don't like him much, because his dad doesn't know about us yet, and... really, even if he did know, this would be awkward. I can't even rationalize this one. I thought everything would be fine, and I knew we'd figure out a way to make this work once our parents came back, but I literally put zero effort into figuring it out before that.

I feel like I probably should have, because now I have no idea what I'm supposed to do. Ethan seems like he has everything figured out, though. I decide to follow his lead.

He sits down first, sliding as far into the booth as he can, and I take a seat next to him, quiet and dainty. I think that's how I'm supposed to be, right? I'm certainly not supposed to cuddle up next to him and share a menu with him and ask him if we can split the food on our plates, and...

Calm down, Ashley! I mentally slap myself, or maybe splash some imaginary cold water into my face. Something! This is difficult.

What am I supposed to do?

Ethan snatches up the menu that the hostess puts in front of him and starts browsing through his options. I barely realize I have a menu of my own. Why is he so calm and relaxed? I guess it's because Ethan always seems calm and relaxed. The perks of being a bad boy?

Well, yes, maybe, but the downside of being a good girl is that you worry about being caught if you do something wrong, and while I don't think Ethan and I are doing anything wrong, I'm still worried about being caught. No real way around that one.

My mom gives me a sympathetic glance before beginning to look at the menu.

"How was your trip?" I ask Ethan's dad and my mom.

I need to get my mind off of Ethan sitting right next to me. It's kind of hard considering I can feel his thigh touching mine, the warmth of his body caressing my leg. It's nice, and I kind of want more, maybe just to reach out and touch his arm or hold his hand for a second, but obviously I can't do that.

"Good!" my mom says. "A little stressful during the day, but we went out to eat at night and tried to relax. It was nice."

"Yeah, it was nice after things settled down," Ethan's dad says with a smile. "During, the day, though... ugh. I felt like I was dealing with a start up company again. We've been in this business for decades and it was like no one knew what to do anymore. I know the industry is changing, but..."

His words trailed off. That was that, apparently.

"How about you two?" Ethan's dad asks, smiling at me and giving Ethan a suspicious look. "Any incidents I should know about?"

Incident? What incident? Like Ethan and I deciding to have a lot of sex with each other?

Really, I don't think that's an incident so much as amazing magic. The things Ethan can do with his hands... his lips... mouth, tongue, fingers... oh, and I shouldn't forget his cock. I mean, honestly, that's a pretty hard thing to forget.

I giggle at myself, for my unintentionally play on words. Cock. Hard? Oh my God, what am I, twelve?

I belatedly realize I'm the only one laughing, which is because, um... I never said any of that out loud. I'm glad I didn't say any of it out loud! Wow, how embarrassing would that be?

Laughing for no reason is pretty embarrassing, too, though.

"It's funny you ask," I say. "Sorry, um... I was laughing about something funny that happened."

"Oh?" Ethan's dad asks.

"Yeah?" Ethan asks.

"Yup, you know, that thing, Ethan?" I say. "I'm sure you remember it better than me."

He gives me a look. It's a very confused look, which I guess I can understand because I literally have no idea what the funny thing is, either. I'm just making this up, but he's supposed to help me here! What good is a boyfriend if he can't make up funny stories to save you from embarrassment? I'm going to have to have a talk with him about this later.

That doesn't save me now, though.

He furrows his brow and looks deep in thought. I'm actually pretty sure any of the funny stories we might have had over the past week are completely inappropriate to discuss at dinner, especially in front of our parents. Mostly because they probably involve us being naked, or having just been naked, or about to be naked, and also um... puzzles. Yes, that's it. Puzzles. Like how you connect the pieces together? Which is um... well, it's sex. There! I said it, except I didn't say it, and Ethan is still looking at me funny.

"I've got nothing, Princess," he says. "Give me a hint?"

"Um, you know? The thing with..." Think, Ashley! Quick! Get it together! "The thing with the pizza, and the drive-in movie place, and Julia?"

There. That's three things. It's the first three things that came to my mind, and we did have pizza a few times last week, and we also went to the drive-in movie place, and my friend Julia came over that one time.

Granted, the first time we had pizza was also the night we accidentally slept together, which started this whole stepbrother with benefits thing, and I gave him a handjob and then we had sex the one and only time we went to the drive-in. When Julia came over that day before we went shopping, she was trying to seduce Ethan, also.

All of these have one thing in common and that's that they're sort of maybe sex-related. Is that funny? Um... I think so, but not in the way I'd hoped.

"Yeah, that time that we bought pizza and then went to the drive-in with your friend Julia," Ethan says. "Great night. Tons of fun."

My mom and Ethan's dad are looking at both of us funny.

"Maybe you had to be there to get it," I say, forcing a laugh, trying to save myself from this horribly awkward situation. "Right, Ethan?"

"Alrighty then..." Ethan's dad says, looking down towards his menu.

"That's a very funny story, you two," my mom says, smiling. "I hope Ethan was on his best behavior with you and your friend."

"That chick's crazy," Ethan chimes in. "Yeah, so Ashley was upstairs getting ready, right? I go to let her in, except I'm shirtless, because--" He pauses, apparently remembering why he was shirtless.

You idiot! Ethan, you can't tell them this story!

"Because you were swimming, I'm sure," my mom says, filling in for him.

"Yeah... yeah, that's exactly what it was. I was swimming, so I was shirtless, and I let Ashley's friend in. She's following me back, and I guess I don't realize it but I have this effect on girls or something and the next thing I know she's trying to put her hand--"

"On Ethan's shoulder!" I shout out, interrupting him. "Ha ha ha! Isn't that... that's funny, huh?"

This isn't funny. None of this is funny! It's disastrous. Ugh!

Wow. I really need to stop doing this. I get myself into too many weird situations and I don't think I like it.

"*Shoulder*, of course," Ethan's dad says, shaking his head. "Ethan, I understand you have a bit of a

7

reputation with women your age, but could you please be respectful with Ashley's friends?"

"Me?" Ethan asks, incredulous. "I didn't do anything with Julia. Fuck. Why do you always jump to conclusions like that?"

"I mean this in the nicest of ways, but it's an easy conclusion to jump to, don't you think?" Ethan's dad says. "I know you've been a lot better lately, what with focusing on school and football. Sowing wild oats is one thing, but would it really kill you to try and have a serious relationship for once? I'm not asking for grandchildren or marriage, but wouldn't it be nice if you had someone you weren't ashamed to bring over for dinner once in awhile?"

I don't know what to say. My mom and I are casualties in this father and son war, I guess. We both sit there quietly while the men battle it out with clenched jaws and glares.

"You don't know me," Ethan says. "Maybe I *have* found someone? What would you say to that?"

"I'd say great!" Ethan's dad says. He laughs, but it's not exactly a nice one. "I'd tell you to invite her to dinner sometime. I don't hate you, Ethan. I'm just looking out for you."

Ethan opens his mouth to say something, but I'm scared of what he might say. I'm worried that he's going to tell his dad about us right here and now, and that it's going to ruin something. I want to tell his dad, I really really do, but not when they're both angry and upset at each other. I think that might make everything worse. I don't think his dad would understand, and I just think he'd get even more upset, which would make Ethan upset, and...

It's just not a good idea.

"Ethan did ask someone to dinner while you were gone," I say suddenly.

Oh my God, what am I doing?

"He did?" my mom asks, confused.

Ethan gives me a look. Don't worry, Mr. Bad Boy. You saved me with a story earlier, so this time it's my turn. I think my story is going to be better than his, though. Really, getting a pizza and going to the drive-in with Julia? That's not even remotely funny! Ugh.

"Yes, actually," I say, matter-of-fact. "It was very sweet. He asked her if she wanted to hang out because her boyfr--" Oh, no, um... if I tell the story that way, it's going to sound exactly like what happened with me and Jake, isn't it? Maybe our parents won't realize it, but that's cutting it too close for me.

"Boy--?" Ethan prompts me.

"Her boy brother," I say.

My mom nods in quiet agreement. "Of course. Not her girl brother. That wouldn't make sense."

Ethan's dad gives my mom a silly look and then laughs. She smiles back at him and pokes her tongue out.

"She was having some problems with her brother," I say, continuing the story. "He told her that he didn't want to see her at all that summer because she wasn't fun. He told her that she needed to learn how to be fun."

"Sounds like someone I know," Ethan's dad says, glancing at Ethan.

"Hey!" Ethan says. "I've been hanging out with Ashley and she's pretty cool. Yeah, yeah, sometimes I'm a jerk, but I wouldn't say shit like that about her."

"Please, Ethan," my mom says. "Mind your mouth. Your father was just joking. Maybe it wasn't the best choice for a joke at the moment, though."

"Sorry," Ethan and his dad say at the same time, grumbling an apology to my mom. It's kind of funny and cute, and it makes me giggle.

"Well, um... so the story I was telling you," I say after a second. "Ethan invited her over for pizza and a movie and it was sweet, and also he made her breakfast in the morning, um... because..."

Oh no, I ruined this. Why did this girl stay over? Well, in the real story, it was me who stayed over, and I stayed over because we had crazy reckless sex and also we live in the same house, so where else was I supposed to stay? Oh, and we were a little tipsy after drinking, which I doubted was a good thing to tell our parents because we're too young to drink.

Maybe my story isn't actually better than Ethan's.

"Look, yeah, she stayed over, and I slept with her," Ethan says, picking up where I left off. "But it's different. I really like this girl."

"It's a little crude, but I guess it's a start, right?" Ethan's dad says.

"It is?" me and my mom ask in tandem. Apparently she's as surprised as I am by this random turn of events.

"He's never had a girl stay the night before, has he?" my stepfather says. "I think we could do with a little less of the sex talk before dinner, but I commend you for taking a step and having a girl stay the night with you, Ethan, and I especially like the fact that you were considerate enough to make her breakfast in the morning."

"Thanks," Ethan says. "I think."

To be honest, I'm not sure if this is a compliment, either. I guess it sounds like one.

"What did you make her for breakfast?" my mom asks.

"Pancakes," Ethan says. "They're her favorite."

"Oh? Ashley, aren't those your favorite, too?" Ethan's dad says. "Did he save any for you?"

I die. I am pretty sure I'm dead right now. I start to choke and cough and splutter and my mom is also dying, apparently. I think it runs in the family. Ethan gives me a look before patting me on the back, except it's kind of a palm slam. Unfortunately that's even worse, because um... it reminds me of...

It's a slap, skin on skin, sort of, and yes, I'm wearing a shirt, but it still reminds me of other sorts of skin on skin slaps, particularly ones involving Ethan and I, which have happened rather frequently lately.

It's sex, alright? It's not the exact same noise or anything but it reminds me of sex, and I think I've just got sex on the mind or something. I'm not good at being a good girl pretending to be a bad girl pretending to be a good girl. This is all too complicated.

Thankfully Ethan's dad is trying to save my mom from choking, too. We aren't even choking on anything, which is probably the worst part about this. Can you choke on ideas and words? I didn't think so before this, but apparently you really can.

A waiter comes up and stands by the table, looking concerned. "Should I get you some water?" he asks. "Is everything alright here?"

We calm down. Sort of. There's no more choking going on, but my face is red and my mom's face is red. Ethan has his hand on my back, rubbing gently. It's nice. I kind of move closer to him, almost nuzzling my cheek against him, but then his dad looks at us and we both freeze.

I notice Ethan and he notices me and we both panic and move back. I look away from him, staring hard at the waiter's shirt, and Ethan does a perfect impression of a mysterious and brooding bad boy, gazing out the window next to him and into the parking lot at nothing in particular.

"Water would be good," I say. "Um... actually, I'm ready to order if everyone else is, too. I think I was just hungry."

"I was choking because I'm hungry, too," my mom says. "I think it's a family trait."

The waiter gives us both a weird look, but Ethan's dad waves his hand, shrugging it off.

"Yes, I think we're all ready to order," my stepdad says.

"Yeah, I'm ready, too," Ethan says. "Sounds good."

# 2 - Ethan

ALRIGHT, SO, WHAT THE FUCK? I'm being serious here, for real: What the fuck?

Everything's confusing as fuck and I don't mean to be huge on the profanity at the moment, but I don't know what to do. It's a really strange place for me.

What do I *want* to do? Well, I'd like to put my arm over Ashley's shoulder while we order our food, and I'd like to maybe give her a quick kiss on the cheek or the lips, and I'd like to whisper stupid shit back and forth with her. I never realized how nice it was to whisper stupid useless junk with someone before I met her. Yeah, you see people doing it, and they smile and giggle or whatever. I don't giggle. What the fuck kind of guy giggles? I've got a reputation to uphold here.

Ashley can giggle, though. I can smile at her giggling. And we can enjoy whispering stupid shit back and forth to each other.

Except, uh... yeah, not with my dad right there. I guess maybe we could do it with her mom here, but my dad and her mom are sort of a package deal, so that's out.

I can't do anything but sit here and look like an asshole. To be honest, it's pretty easy to do.

Then she wants me to tell a story, though? What the fuck are you doing to me, Princess? Do I look like I'm some professional storyteller? Stephen King or something?

Yeah so I told a story. Apparently it was really bad. Who knew?

And then she tells a story and it's pretty good, but now I guess I'm dating some other girl. Yeah, yeah, I catch on quick that the other girl is actually Ashley, but my dad doesn't know that.

This is fucked up is what I'm trying to tell you, and I don't like it.

Also, you know what's worse? I ordered a burger with onion rings and I asked for it rare. Do you know what I have in front of me right now?

They got the onion rings. I have a burger. Is the burger rare? I asked for it rare, so you would think so, but this is not a rare burger. It's medium rare at best, and it really pisses me off when restaurants try to pull that shit. I asked for it rare, you've got some stupid disclaimer on your menu about undercooked food, and I totally get that, but give me what I want, not what's safe for me.

Do you know who I am? I'm kind of a bad boy here, and I deal with unsafe on a daily basis. Maybe not daily, but at least once a week I probably do something stupid, so if the only thing I do wrong this week is get sick from an undercooked burger, I'd consider that a huge accomplishment.

This is why I don't get a motorcycle, by the way. Pretty fucking sure I'd mess that up bad. I'm a bad boy, but I'm not an idiot. I can still look cool in a convertible. Probably cooler, because who the fuck rides a motorcycle shirtless?

Who drives a convertible sports car shirtless? Me! Bam!

Yeah, so, that's where we're at. Eating. Easy, right?

Nah. It's never that easy.

Ashley got some chicken fingers platter that she dips into honey mustard sauce, plus some french fries. Except she stole some of my onion rings and trade them for french fries. What the fuck?

My dad gave me a look after that. I had to do something.

"Yeah, just steal my food," I tell her. "Go right ahead, Princess."

Real sarcastic and snarky, right? Ashley sticks her tongue out at me and gives me a look. Holy fuck, I want to kiss her so bad right then. Kiss her and shove my hand down her pants. *Romantically*, though. I'm pretty sure you can grope someone with romantic intentions. If not, that's dumb.

"Thank you, Ethan," she says, after I glare at her.

I grumble something. I don't know what. Doesn't matter, it's not important. Everyone goes back to their food. I bite into my burger, though I'm none too happy about it. Yeah, I could send it back, but then I've got to wait for more food and I'm hungry here. I chomp down on a french fry to try and cool my anger, and that's about when more "what the fuck?" stuff starts to happen.

There's a hand. It's a hand I know. It's Ashley's hand. Want to know where it is? Right on top of my cock. What a fucking tease.

She puts her hand on my thigh while acting innocent, dipping a chicken finger into her honey mustard sauce. When she brings it to her mouth and takes a bite, her hand slides up my thigh, towards my crotch, and she just lays it there. Sort of. Grabbing, too.

Ashley's really grabby, actually. It's not just me. Yes, I can't keep my hands off of her, but this is mutual grabbiness going on. I am not the only one to blame. She can't keep her hands off of me, either.

Thankfully the table is high enough where no one can really see what's going on, but Little Miss Perfect over here is definitely squeezing my cock. I was trying to restrain myself, but she's not helping, and if I didn't have my pants on, I'd have a full on erection right about now. Pants are the only thing holding that bad boy back.

Kind of wish that was what was going on, though. Erections are great. I was hungry for food, but I'm hungry for other stuff, too. Kind of like how you tell yourself you could really go for a burger right about now? That's me, and I really could go for a burger, which is why I got one, but I could also really go for a handjob right about now. How amazing would it be to get a handjob and eat a burger at the same time? Amazing as fuck, that's what that'd be.

It's not going to happen, though.

I try to shift away, but she's got an obvious advantage here. It takes two hands to eat a burger of this magnitude, and it only takes one hand for her to eat everything on her plate. Meaning, she has a free hand available to molest me. Which is what she's doing.

My cock stiffens even more, straining to get free. Fuck! It's hard to concentrate. I bring my burger to my mouth and go to take a bite, but I almost miss. How dumb would I look with ketchup and burger grease all over my face? Why do you do this to me, Princess? I give her a sidelong glare, and I know she sees it, but she just ignores me.

I put the burger down, moving towards the onion rings. Two can play at this game, and I do not like to lose. Just as I manage to slip my free hand under the table and make my move, uh...

Holy fuck, she doesn't play fair, does she? Wow. I don't even know what to say anymore.

She clears her throat, attracting attention. Her mom and my dad look up from their food and their quiet conversation with each other about some business junk. All eyes on Ashley, which means it's a lot harder for me to shove my hand between her thighs and tease her like she's teasing me.

Why am I dating this girl? I'm supposed to be the one teasing her and getting what I want. It's not supposed to be the other way around. I'll give her what she wants when I'm good and ready to do it. That's how this used to work. She's changed the rules completely.

I guess that's how this started in the first place. This is just one of those invisible rules that no one ever talks about. *Ashley's Rule.*

"Where are we going camping?" she asks.

I don't know if she actually cares or if she's just trying to keep me from groping her. Either way, my groping is put to an abrupt stop.

"There's this campground that Ethan and I used to go to sometimes when he was younger," my dad says. "It's out in the woods, more of a real roughing it type of place. They've got an electrical outlet for each site, but it's only enough to power something small. Usually for emergency use. Other than that, it's firewood and true outdoorsmanship."

"I hope there's showers and water, though?" my stepmom asks.

"At the office," my dad says. "There's a pool up there, too, but there's a lake nearby that's nicer. The showers are paid use. I don't know how much it costs now, but it used to be a quarter per minute, so you learn to move quick."

"It's more fun to just go swimming," I say. It's only then that I realize Ashley really doesn't play fair, because, uh... hello? Her hand is still squeezing my cock.

Wow. Seriously, wow. Just wow.

"Yeah, that's what we used to do," my dad says. "I guess it's not the same as a real shower, but it's more refreshing than one. It's an entirely different world there. You can walk for miles in the woods and never see anyone, or spend an entire day down at the lake. You can swim or fish. We'd need a license for fishing, but it's easy to get. If we do that, we can even cook what we catch over the fire later."

"It sounds like a lot of fun," Ashley says, her hand gently massaging my throbbing erection. "I've never been fishing before."

"Ethan could teach you?" my stepmom offers.

I will literally agree to anything right now, if only Ashley would stop teasing me. That, or just finish me off. Let's go somewhere private, Princess... I'll show you the consequences of what you've started.

She eases up, which I take as a good sign, except, nah, then she keeps going with her foot. Tapping at mine, rubbing up and down.

Ugh. Holy fucking... *ugh*. At least a foot's better than a cock, I guess.

"Yes," I say, because everyone's staring at me now. "Yeah, I can teach you how to fish. Could be fun."

"That's very nice of you," my stepmom says.

"It really is, Ethan," Ashley says, smiling at me. "I appreciate it a lot. I think it'd be fun for you to teach me..."

She trails off there, and I guess to the average person it'd seem like that's the end of her sentence, but I'm pretty sure this is some sort of play on words. You know how this all started? Stepbrother with benefits, I was going to help her and teach her stuff. That was even one of the rules. *This is supposed to be fun. I don't care what you've done before, Princess. This is about what you want to do now.*

I wanted to teach her so many things and I still do, but to be honest, fishing didn't exactly cross my mind before. It's barely even on my mind now. I can't stop thinking about...

Yeah, well, you know what I'm thinking about. Let's not even pretend I'm not.

"There's the hot spring, too," I say, quick, because I'm not thinking straight.

"Oh, yeah, I almost forgot about that," my dad says.

"What's that?" Ashley asks.

"It's nothing too out there. There's a natural hot spring a little further past the lake. It's a hike to get there, but once you are, it's nice. Supposedly it has magical properties, or that's what the campground owner says. I really doubt it. It's a nice place, though. Kind of like the jacuzzi at home, but natural and with the added bonus of minerals in the water."

"Yeah, it's cool," I say. "I could show you sometime if you want?"

By that, I mean I can't stop thinking about a couple of the previous times Ashley and I were in the jacuzzi, which basically ended in a lot of sex. You think a natural hot spring spot would be any different? I don't. Sex, with the added benefit of it being outdoor sex. Kinky as fuck? Yeah, let's go skinny dipping at the hot spring, Princess. My intentions are not even remotely pure.

I guess we could get caught doing that, but seriously the hot spring is basically out in the middle of nowhere. If we go really early or really late, we'd have it to ourselves, and...

Yeah, you're in trouble, Princess. Really really really big trouble.

Ashley just smiles. I don't think she's oblivious, but she doesn't know what kind of beast she's awoken. Or she does, and she's looking forward to it. I think it's the latter and I'm happy to oblige.

Chat goes back to idle stuff after that, nothing too serious. I try to eat my burger while this insane girl next to me keeps playing footsie with me. I nudge her back. I never really considered this as an option, but it's kind of fun. Bad boys don't play footsie with girls, you know? It's too cutesy, not really my style.

I guess it's my style now. What the fuck again? Dammit, Ashley!

"I need to go to the bathroom really quick," she says all of a sudden, excusing herself from her food.

She's on the outside of the booth, so it's easy for her to get up. I stare after her, my foot suddenly bereft, no longer in the company of another foot, lonely as fuck. She smiles to my dad and her mom, and then she turns to me, giving me some mischievous smirk. She's having fun with this, just teasing and toying with me.

I've created a monster. A sexy as fuck monster, but she's still a monster.

She sashays through the restaurant to the restrooms down a hall in the back. I watch her go, because, *that ass*. Pretty easy to watch, if I'm being honest. I pick up an onion ring and stuff it in my mouth, chewing away, thinking of the teasing frustration I'm going to have to deal with as soon as she gets back.

We're halfway done eating, so that's halfway through the meal, and then we can leave. That's if we don't get dessert, though. Fuck, I hadn't thought about dessert. I take another bite of my burger, dealing with the logistics in my head. There could be after dinner coffee, too. Or talking. Maybe a shared appetizer? You usually get appetizers before the meal, but sometimes they're nice for after if you just want to hang out and talk.

Do we usually hang out and talk? Uh... nah. Not really, but I feel like now is different. Ashley and I have been away at college for most of the year, and then our parents were gone for most of the first week we were back, so there's a potential reason for more idle chit chat.

Idle chit chat really fucking sucks when you just want to get up, go home, drag your stepsister upstairs to her room, or yours, throw her on the bed, and fuck her for hours. Generally I like idle chit chat, but not now.

Wait.

Wait wait wait

Seriously, just wait a second.

I'm missing something.

This is important as fuck.

Ashley went to the bathroom. Our parents are not in the bathroom. I've been to this restaurant before, and in particular the bathrooms. They're one person per room, one male and one female bathroom. Ashley is in the female one.

Did she lock the door?

"Hey," I say. "I've got to use the bathroom, too. I'll be right back."

Nod nod nod, make this official. My dad shrugs, grunts, goes back to his food. Ashley's mom smiles at me as I slide out of the booth. If she suspects anything, she doesn't say it. Shit, I wouldn't suspect anything, either. This is a kind of crazy thing for me to do, but I feel like if I didn't do it I'd have my official bad boy membership card revoked.

Fuck, you know what I should do? Get a bad boy membership card. Then when Ashley tries to pull her teasing shit, I can just whip that out, show it to her, and then have my way with her. Yeah, I could do that without the card, but the card seems like it'd make it even better. Extra legit, right?

I strut through the restaurant, trying to keep my cool, just relaxing. I head towards the hall to the restrooms. I hope to fuck there's not a line. I can't exactly stroll into the women's room if there's someone waiting outside, now can I? I guess I could, but that might cause some issues, and I don't want to deal with that right now.

I want to deal with something else. Namely, the partly erect cock throbbing between my legs.

I get to the hall. No one is there, no waiting, nothing. I go up to the door to the women's room, grab the handle, twist it, and...

Fuck yeah! Unlocked! I open it quick and then shut the door behind me. A surprised looking Ashley standing in front of the mirror and inspecting herself opens her mouth to scream, but I rush in, grab her, spin her around, and clamp my hand over her mouth. I back up slowly to the door with her in tow and lock it.

That's it. I'm done.

I kiss her neck, slow and soft at first, but faster and faster with each kiss. Harder, louder. I move my hand away from her mouth when it's obvious she's not going to scream anymore. She surprises me by moaning instead.

"Ethan, what are you doing?" she asks, her voice a sultry gasp.

"What'd you think you were doing during dinner?" I ask her. "It's all fun and games until someone gets an erection, huh?"

"That's not how the saying goes!" she says, giggling and squirming in my arms.

"You think you can just tease me like that without some repercussions, Princess?"

"Mhm," she says, a silly smirk on her lips. "You were talking about anticipation earlier so I wanted to get you worked up."

"What kind of good girl *are* you?" I ask. "That's not even something good girls do, Princess."

"I'm a very *bad* good girl," she says, pouting. "I think maybe I need to be punished, Ethan." More pouting.

Holy fuck, this is doing things to me, you don't even know. I pull her closer, wrapping my hand around her stomach, grinding against her ass. She wiggles back against me, grinding even more.

"You had your hands all over me," I say. "I think it's only fair I do the same, don't you?"

She nods fast. "Mhm, I do."

Yeah, well, that's all I need. That's all it takes. I wrestle with the button of her shorts and unzip them quick, then rip them down her legs. Her panties, too. Gone, down, resting near her ankles. I push her forward so she's bending over, then I move to the side behind her. I rub my hand along her ass, feeling her delicious, sensual curves.

I tap her ass lightly, just a feeler, and she whimpers and squirms. I do it a little more, harder, but not too hard, then I rub lightly. I move down, teasing her pussy with my fingers. She's wet as fuck already, and I kind of just want to dip two fingers in and drag them out slowly, then lick them and taste her arousal for myself, but I've got some punishment to do here.

I spank her again, then once more. Just light and playful, sexy as fuck. She whimpers and wiggles. I've spanked girls before, but uh... only during sex? You know, when I'm taking them from behind, a quick ass smack. I don't know if this is the same as that. I guess a quick smack on the ass when a girl is walking away is kind of a spank, too. I kind of like this, though. The difference is intriguing as fuck. I could definitely get used to it.

Nothing too insane, let's not go crazy here. I'm just saying I wouldn't be opposed to bending Ashley over sometime and giving her a few quick spanks before fucking the shit out of her.

Or making love. Whatever. I can be gentle, too. Roughly gentle. That's a thing. I just made it up. Fuck off.

I don't know if it's her or me but I can't take this anymore. I drive two fingers into her slick, wet sex, thrusting hard. She's still bent over, but she gasps and almost stands up at the sudden feeling of my fingers inside her. I pull my fingers out and she settles back down a little, but then I thrust them in again. This time she's ready for it, at least a little bit, and she holds her position. Her knees wobble, nearly buckling, but she manages to keep her balance.

"Ethan," she whimpers. "I'm sorry for teasing you during dinner..."

"Do you know how much I want to fuck you right now?" I tell her.

"You should," she says. Then, the kicker. "I dare you!"

"Nah," I say, pulling my fingers out and teasing at her clit. Her knees really do buckle that time and she almost falls over, but I catch her. "You're not the only one that can tease here, Princess."

I hold her up, dragging her to her feet again. She's still got her panties and shorts around her ankles, but that doesn't matter. I wrap my arm around her, keeping her on her feet like that, and my other hand nestles between her legs. I tease and torment her clit, then run my fingers up and down her slick labia, back to her clit. This isn't exactly smooth and sensual here, but it's not too rough.

I have a plan, I'm a man on a mission.

I can see her in the mirror, even though her back is to me. Her eyes roll into the back of her head and her mouth opens, lips parted a little. I pick up the pace, focusing solely on her clit now, this beautiful fucking button. Push it in just the right way and you get a surprise in the form of an orgasm.

Fuck, I love watching her orgasm. It's truly a thing of beauty. Art or something, that's what that is.

She's close. She's breathing heavier, her stomach clenches. I can feel her body tensing beneath me and her legs almost giving way, but with my support she keeps her ground. A little faster... a little more...

I stop right when she's on the edge. Just stop. Delicate and nice, like a classy gentleman, I stoop down and grab her panties, then pull them up her legs. When they're in place, like panties should be, I go for her shorts, too.

She realizes what's going on then and almost stops me. Almost, except I'm stronger and faster than her, so those shorts are back, zippered, and buttoned up before she can spin around and confront me.

"Ethan Colton, what do you think you're doing!" she practically roars at me.

"Hey, we're in the bathroom at a public restaurant, remember?" I say.

Her eyes widen, only now seeming to realize uh... yeah, what we're doing is kind of fucked up no matter how you put it. This isn't even just the stepbrother and stepsister thing, but having sex in the bathroom of a restaurant is... well, I'm a bad boy, it's what I do.

"Why did you stop?" she whispers, with a little bit of a whimper added in there for good measure.

"I think it was that anticipation thing," I say, quoting what she said before back to her. "I'm practicing."

"That's stupid," she says. "You're stupid."

"They say practice makes perfect. Maybe I should do it again when we get home?"

"Are you seriously just going to bring me to the brink of orgasm and then stop? I don't like that."

"Yeah, well, I hadn't thought about it like that, but I don't like it, either. I want to make you cum so hard you can't even think straight."

I think we're at an impasse. How do we get past this? If we both get into a teasing war that never ends in orgasm for anyone, I'm pretty sure that's worse than the end of the world. Seriously, I'd rather deal with zombies or something. Sounds a million times easier.

"Alright," she says. "I'll stop teasing you. For now."

"What's that mean?" I ask. "I don't like how you ended that. *For now?*"

"I mean, it is kind of fun, don't you think? A *little* teasing?"

"Yeah, I mean, a little is alright. Like... *a little* a little."

"This needs to be a rule," she says. "This is important."

"Are you being serious right now?" I ask. I really can't tell. Sometimes I think she's crazy.

"Dreadfully serious," she says with a straight face. Mostly straight, but then she starts to smile and laugh. "I guess it's not that serious, but I still think it should be a rule."

"Alright, tell me what it is," I say. "I'm ready for it."

"Rule number nineteen," she says. "Teasing and anticipation should always lead to future pleasure. We're each allowed to give each other one moment of intense excitement and build up, but that's it. Just one! And then the next time is the real thing."

"So... next time?" I ask.

"Mhm," she murmurs, biting her bottom lip and nodding. "I won't tease you again and you won't tease me again, because the next time is..."

*Aw yeah.* This sounds amazing. I am pretty sure this is amazing as fuck.

"When we get home, though," she says.

Shit. "Fuck."

"I'd really like to right now but you have to admit it's kind of inappropriate and not a good place."

"I can do it standing up," I say. "I have no issue with that."

"It's not that!" she says, giggling. "Don't you think our parents are going to wonder why we've been gone for so long?"

"Fuck," I say. This is why Ashley is the smart one, I guess. She knows what's up.

"*Fuck...* me when we get home?" she says.

"I guarantee you that I'll be doing that," I say. Two orgasms for the price of one, guaranteed or your money back. Maybe a few more if Ashley's feeling feisty.

"Alright," she says, blushing and shy. I don't know why she does this, because I don't think she has any right to be shy about it anymore, but to be honest it's cute as fuck and I love it. I hope she never stops.

"I guess I'll let myself out, then," I say, trying to be a gentleman before I change my mind and tear off her shorts again.

"I'm all done, too," she says.

"Well, alright then," I say.

Chivalrous and gallant, the perfect bad boy knight, I sweep open the bathroom door for her. It's supposed to be nice and awesome and great, except there's an elderly woman standing just outside the bathroom waiting to use it. She blinks when she sees me standing there, and her eyes go to the sign on the wall next to the door. She blinks again when she sees Ashley there with me.

Why does this stuff happen to me? I don't know. I blame Ashley. It's really all her fault to begin with. This wouldn't have happened if she didn't feel the need to grab my crotch during dinner.

The old woman opens her mouth as if to scream. Shit. Think think think. This is important. Uh...

"It's cool," I say. "She's my sister. I was helping her out with a wardrobe malfunction."

# 3 - Ashley

Wow. Really, Ethan? Um... wow.

First off, Ethan is my walking wardrobe malfunction. Whenever I'm around him, I seem to end up losing my clothes. It's a serious problem.

Also, I'm pretty sure it's not even a wardrobe malfunction when he's the one trying to take off my clothes. That's something that takes active thought and manipulation. A malfunction would indicate that it happened by accident, and this is definitely not that.

This is really bad, though, isn't it? This woman is going to scream and call attention to us and I have no idea how to explain why Ethan was in the bathroom with me. Also, ugh. I understand why he said the sister thing, but it's weird.

I totally understand that I've done this to him with the brother thing, and maybe my brother thing was worse than his sister thing, but I don't know. I really don't know! Ugh.

The woman doesn't scream, though. Instead, she starts to smile.

"That's so nice of you, young man," she says.

"Yeah, I know," Ethan says, grinning. "I'm kind of awesome like that."

"Seriously?" I ask. I should be happy, but I don't know why she believes him.

"You're lucky to have a brother like him," the woman says to me. "Just be careful, you two. Someone else might not be as understanding. People make a lot of assumptions in life, and you don't want them getting the wrong idea."

"Oh no, of course not," I say, nodding.

"Yeah, wouldn't want that," Ethan agrees.

"Alright, well, if you don't mind, I really do need to use the restroom," the woman says.

Ethan steps aside, and, with a flourish of his hands he offers her use of the restroom. I sneak out and move to the side, too, letting the woman go in.

Once she's behind closed doors, I glare at him. "You're so stupid," I say.

"I'm stupid?" he asks. "You're the one who needs to get her clothes checked."

"My clothes would be fine if *someone's* hands didn't keep grabbing at them."

"That's what they all say, Princess."

"Ethan, no one says that. That's not something anyone says."

"You just said it," he points out.

"I don't like you."

"Wow, real good girlfriend you are."

"Shut up!"

He grins at me, and I almost melt. Almost! Not quite. I need to be a little angry at him. I don't know why anymore. Just because.

I huff and glare at him and say, "I hope my food isn't cold. If it is, I'm blaming you."

"Sure thing," he says. "Whatever helps you sleep at night."

I start to walk down the hall back to the restaurant proper. "I don't know what--"

Smack!

He spanked me! He smacked my butt!

I spin around and stare at him, wide-eyed and open-mouthed. Ethan grins at me, silly and fun. I wish he wouldn't look at me like that. I just want to hug and kiss him now, which I'm pretty sure is wildly inappropriate here. I *know* it's wildly inappropriate!

Ethan makes me want to do a lot of wildly inappropriate things. They're kind of a lot of fun.

"Ethan!" I whisper loudly at him. "Be good!"

"You're the good girl, Princess," he says. "Why don't you just keep on walking?"

"Rule number nineteen!" I tell him, jumping away and down the hall before he can spank me again. "This isn't allowed!"

We half walk regular, half chase and run from each other down the hall until we get back to the main restaurant area. Then we walk mostly regularly, except I'm kind of scared Ethan's going to smack my butt again. He wouldn't, right? Um... I would not take that bet, no matter the odds.

I keep my hands behind me, partly hovered over my butt, trying to look regular. This doesn't even look anywhere close to regular, does it? I turn over my shoulder and look at Ethan, and he's just watching me, grinning, almost laughing.

"Shut up," I tell him.

"I didn't even say anything," he says.

We make it back to the table without incident. Ethan slides in, acting like he owns it, and I scurry in next to him.

"Was everything alright?" my mom asks, raising her eyebrow at me.

"Um... yes?" I answer. That's an answer, right?

"Little Miss Perfect over here clogged up the toilet," Ethan says. "I had to give her a hand."

He did not! Or did he? Yes, his hand was involved... but I'm pretty sure that's not what this means at all. In Ethan Bad Boy World, that's probably exactly what it means, though. *Need a plumber? How about I fingerfuck you instead?*

He's so terrible and rude and bad and I love him and he's my boyfriend.

I don't know what that makes me, then.

I pick up one of my chicken fingers and dip it into the honey mustard sauce. It's still warm. Mmm yum! Ethan picks up his burger and takes a bite, too. Our parents are mostly done eating now, so it's just us.

"Do you want a chicken finger?" I ask Ethan.

"Yeah, sure," he says. "You want a bite of my burger?"

I nod, quick. He holds it out for me to take a bite, and I do. I give him a chicken finger, too. He dips it into the honey mustard sauce and eats it.

And um... oh my God, this isn't how we're supposed to act, is it? Eek...

Ethan's dad gives us a strange look. It's the sort of contemplative curious look that says he's trying to figure out what's going on. I do not want him figuring out what's going on. I need to do something to throw him off our trail.

"Don't get too used to this," I tell Ethan. "I'm only sharing with you because you helped me with the toilet."

Ethan gives me a look that basically says what the fuck do I care?

This seems to work. For now. Ethan's dad shakes his head at us.

"You two really need to learn how to get along," he says. "It's a work in progress, I guess."

"Oh, I'm sure they'll figure it out soon enough," my mom says.

Really, Mom? Really?

# 4 - Ethan

WE ALL CAME IN ONE CAR to the restaurant, so obviously that's the way we're getting home, but this is kind of awkward. My dad's driving, Ashley's mom is in the passenger seat, and I'm in the back with Ashley. You know what happens in the back seat of a car? When you're with a girl you really want to just... do back seat of a car things with?

Yeah, well, that's about where I'm at right now, except with our parents in the front, there's no chance that's going to work. Also, what the fuck is with rule number nineteen. It seemed like a good idea at the time, but we've both used up our allowance of teasing each other without finishing the deed, so we're just kind of sitting here, doing nothing, looking at each other now and again.

I'd be down to uh... fuck if I know. Touch her thigh or something? How does this even work? I guess it's better if we don't do anything, because one wrong look from my dad and it's done. No clue how to even explain that, and I don't even want to try right now.

It won't matter for long. We're driving home.

Except then we're not. Holy fuck, why does everything have to be so complicated here?

My dad pulls into the mall parking lot and parks at the entrance to the food court. Uh... we just ate?

"I figured we should stock up on supplies for the camping trip," he says, turning the car off. "We've got some of our old gear at home, Ethan, but there's not enough for the ladies."

"I'd like to pick up some clothes, too," my stepmom says. "Ashley, do you want to come with me and Ethan can go with his father?"

"Sure," she says. "I think that's a good idea."

Does anyone ask me what I think? No, probably not. Probably a good idea they don't, too. I just can't stop thinking about Ashley, which uh... yeah, not going to say that to anyone. I'd say it to Ashley, but I'm pretty sure she already knows.

Yeah, fine, alright. I get it. Mall. We're getting out. Camping gear. Got it.

I get out of the car and get in line next to my dad. Ashley's with her mom. We head into the entrance together, but then me and my dad take a left towards the sporting goods store and Ashley and her mom go right to some clothes place or something. I have no idea.

"What do we have to grab?" I ask. I want to get this done, the faster the better.

"Not sure our old tent is holding up anymore," my dad says. "Plus, I'm sure you and Ashley will want your own tents, and I think we should get a bigger one for me and her mom. We'll check out a few other essentials over there, too. Oh, and a pair of extra fishing rods just in case we all want to go together. Our old ones should still be fine, and I doubt we need anything fancy. They'll have worms at one of the corner stores down there."

"Got it," I say. "Tents and rods."

We head to the tents first. This is going to take a little more time than the fishing rods. You know how many types of tents there are? Yeah, uh... a lot. When the fuck did camping get so confusing? I remember back in the day we just had this tent me and my dad shared together, some other gear we kept in the car, and that was about it.

Now they've got tents that are like mini houses, with multiple rooms. Seriously? It's a fucking tent. Why does a tent need three rooms, a screen porch, and a den? I literally can't even begin to wrap my mind around that one.

There's dome tents, or square tents, rectangle tents. Tents tall enough to stand in, or ones made just for sleeping and laying down. I can't quite figure out why you'd want to stand in a tent, to be honest. When I'm camping, I'm either outdoors doing outdoors stuff, or I'm sleeping in the tent. It's not like you go around the campsite and invite people over for a dinner party with wine tasting in your standing room tent. Oh, don't forget it's got multiple rooms. Maybe just bring a dining table and have a full on banquet in your tent?

People these days, for real.

My dad picks out a decent sized one for him and my stepmom, then turns to me to confer about the rest.

"What do you think?" he asks.

I think this is dumb, Dad. "We can just get one other tent," I say. "I don't think we need two."

"Yeah, right. You and Ashley sharing a tent?" my dad asks, chuckling. "That's got to be a recipe for disaster."

I grunt and clench my jaw, but refrain from saying something stupid. I shouldn't have suggested it in the first place. I wasn't really thinking straight, I guess. I'm just not that excited about having to hide this shit after the week Ashley and I have been through. I was kind of hoping we wouldn't have to do that, but uh... yeah, well...

Maybe when we get to the campground we can talk and figure this out, but for now I've got to pick out two tents. Fuck.

"I don't know, how about this one?" I offer, pointing to a respectable dome tent. It's nice enough, just regular, nothing crazy. Good to sleep in, big enough to lay down and stretch out.

"Sure," my dad says, smiling. "Looks good. I think Ashley will be fine with that."

We get everything situated there and then head over to the fishing rods. This should be easy. Pick two and get out. I hope Ashley and her mom are almost finished up with clothing shopping, too. I think that might be wishful thinking, because women and clothing shopping is uh... yeah... I'm not even going to get into that.

As we're walking down the aisle to the fishing rods, my dad says, "I know things have been a little rough with you two, and I'm sure school and everything has been hard sometimes, too. I wish I could have been there when you got back. I didn't want to just leave you alone like that for a week, you know?"

"Dad, it's cool. I can handle myself," I say.

"I know," he says. "I worry, that's all. I'm sure it wasn't any better after what happened with Ashley, either."

I freeze. After... wait, does he know? Nah, that makes no sense. "Huh?"

"Her boyfriend breaking up with her," my dad says. "I don't know the full details, but I know you're not really good at dealing with break up business."

Thanks a lot, Dad. I'm pretty sure that's his way of saying I'm a dick for ditching girls in the past, and yeah, I guess I kind of am, but I tried to tell them all it wasn't serious to begin with. Is that really my fault, then? I'm trying to be different now. I know about break ups, I just don't like being involved with them.

"I just mean that I think it would have been easier with her mother around to talk with her, and I don't know what happened between you and Ashley while we were gone, but I imagine there was a lot of stress and heightened emotions. You both probably said some things you didn't mean and I know how you two love to argue, so I doubt her break up with her boyfriend helped matters any."

"Dad, her ex-boyfriend is a dick," I say. There's no real way around that one. What else am I supposed to say? "I'm pretty sure Ashley realizes that."

I know she does. I didn't need to punch the stupid fuck in the face for her to know it, but I hope I helped her realize it a little more when I did. Fuck. I want to punch him again. Seriously.

"Look," my dad says. "I'm not saying he's not a jerk, but you've been known to play the field a bit, yourself. I'm not sure you should be judging anyone."

"It's completely different," I say. I don't want to start an argument, but I'm totally going to start one if he keeps this up. I'm not even remotely similar to Ashley's douchebag ex. I'd never pull the shit he tried to pull.

"How's it different?" my dad asks.

He doesn't want to know, he just wants to do that thing he does where he tries to get me to see his side of things. Yeah, well, your side is wrong this time, Dad. I don't know how to tell you that without completely fucking everything up and saying something I'll regret, though.

"They were dating for months, first off," I say. "That's kind of serious, don't you think? And then he went and treated her like an asshole."

"Serious relationships are difficult," my dad says. "Have you ever had a serious relationship, Ethan? I'm not trying to be mean here, but it's not something you can understand unless you've done it. Sometimes people say and do things that they don't exactly mean. It can make or break the bond two people have, but if they push through it they can become stronger."

Oh, yeah? So Jake tried to blackmail Ashley but he didn't mean it? It was a mistake? And if she went along with him and acted as his sex toy for a weekend, and they pushed through it, they could have a stronger, tighter relationship than ever before?

Fuck off, Dad. I mean that in the nicest of ways, but he seriously has no fucking clue what he's talking about in this case.

"Listen," I say, trying to be diplomatic. This is new, and I'm only bothering to try it because of Ashley. "If I were dating Ashley--" Fuck! I fucked this up already, didn't I? "I mean, if I were dating a girl like Ashley," I correct myself. "I'd never treat her like he did. I would never say or do the things he did."

There. That's good, right? He doesn't have to know the specifics.

My dad gives me a weird look, and I'm not sure if it's because of the "If I were dating Ashley" thing or something else.

Nah, it's something else, apparently. "Ethan, you've been treating her like that for years. When her mom and I came home, you two were having an argument in the game room. I love you, son, and I want the best for you, and I want you to find a girl you can be serious about, but you've got a really bad track record. Frankly, if I were Ashley's father, I wouldn't want you dating my daughter, either."

Wow. Really, Dad? Really? Wow. Just... holy fucking wow.

What can I even say to that? Because he is, you know? Her father, I mean. Stepfather, but in this case it's practically the same thing. There's underlying issues here or something, and he's said his piece. He doesn't know, and I guess now he can never know. He doesn't agree. He wouldn't understand. He would not accept me dating Ashley, because he literally just said he wouldn't.

I guess that's it. I don't know what to say. I want to say something. I consider just being straight with him and telling him that I *am* dating Ashley. We've been dating for a few days now. It's going good, actually. That argument in the game room? Yeah, that was fake, because her mom was supposed to tell you before you two got back, but she didn't. Did you really want to know I was fucking Ashley on the pool table right before you two got home? Uh... pretty sure you didn't! I didn't want to tell you that, either. I didn't mean for it to be something anyone found out about, and, yeah, I got a little excited and made a mistake there, but I make a lot of mistakes.

I get it, Dad. I'm a fuck up. I fuck everything up. I fucked this up.

I don't want to, though. I want to make this work. I...

Just fuck it. I don't have to explain shit to anyone.

"Can we just get some fishing rods and get out of here?" I say.

"Yeah," my dad says, sighing. "I didn't mean to get into that conversation with you. I'm just looking out for you, Ethan."

"I get it, Dad," I say. "It's no big deal, alright?"

It's kind of a big deal to me.

Mia Clark

# 5 - *Ashley*

Oooh, this one is cute," my mom says, holding up a... shirt?

"Mom, it's a t-shirt," I say. "I mean, I guess it's cute? It looks the same as all the other shirts, though."

"It's a cute camping shirt, Ashley," my mom says. "Sometimes you need to choose between cute and utilitarian, but I think this one is both."

I laugh. "Really? I think it's nice, but it's just a shirt."

"Well, I'm going to get it!" she says, lifting her head up, proud.

"And I'm going to get..." I snatch up a shirt. It's mostly regular, but I do like it. It's cute in its own way, and it's a bit tighter fitting, so it won't hang loose around my upper body. Not um... too tight, but tight enough? I want to look nice around Ethan still, even if we're camping.

"I approve," my mom says with a nod.

We pick out a few more things, just essentials. I have regular clothes, but obviously camping is going to be a bit dirtier, right? Some of what I have at home isn't exactly well-suited for roughing it, so the clothes here will be good. It's kind of weird to me to buy something specifically for camping when I don't think we'll be going camping for very long or very often. Actually...

"How long are we going to be camping?" I ask.

My mom considers it for a second. "I'm not entirely sure, but I think it's a week. Maybe two. I believe we're just going to play it by ear. Why? Do you have a date planned with your secret lover?"

"Mom," I say, staring at her blankly.

"What? I'm just curious. Do you?"

"I don't know?" I tell her. Um... Ethan, do we? He's not here to ask. Secret date with my secret lover? It sounds like it could be fun, actually. "We haven't really planned anything out too much. We just go have fun in the moment."

"I understand," my mom says with a smile. "You really should plan something sometime, though. It can be a lot of fun. I don't know if I ever told you this, but Ethan's good at planning out activities. He used to help me with figuring out what we were going to do when we went on business trips with you two during high school."

"Wait, what? Really?" I did not know this. Honestly, I never would have suspected this, either.

"Oh, yes," my mom says, grinning ear to ear now. "Part of it was because he just wanted to get out of the hotel room. I know you stayed behind during the days to do your homework, and I think that's fine, dear, but Ethan's got a knack for finding things to do, and while his father was in meetings or doing business things, Ethan and I would plan out the trip. I think he had ulterior motives, because he liked to do his own thing during the days, but most of what we did after that in the evenings was a joint effort planned by the two of us."

"You never told me that," I say. I don't know why it would have made a difference, but I think I might have liked to know.

My mom shrugs. "I didn't mean to keep it a secret," she says. "I guess it never came up. He's good at it, though. If you two plan together, I bet you could come up with some really fun and exciting dates."

"It's not like our dates haven't been fun and exciting," I say. "They have. I like them a lot. I know that, um... well, we haven't gone anywhere too crazy yet, but I..." I don't know how to say this or explain it without sounding dumb, so I just stop.

"You don't have a lot of experience with dating," my mom says, understanding. "If I had to guess, Ethan doesn't, either. You're both used to different things and different types of situations, but I think that's a good thing, too."

"How?" I ask. I kind of really want to know. My mom seems so good at this, like she understands everything. I'm good at book smarts and things like that, but this is entirely different and new to me.

"Relationships aren't always about being the same," my mom says. "A lot of the time it's about being different, and learning about each other's differences. When you do something new and different with someone, you learn a lot about them. I think it brings you closer. Everything you do brings you closer in its own way, but a good mix of different things can give you a full appreciation of who exactly you're with."

"Ethan's really nice," I say without thinking. That um... well, no, he's a bad boy, too? "I know he's sometimes not nice, but he's really nice to me, too. It's hard to explain. He's really patient, but I feel like I can do more when I'm with him, if that makes sense? Like, it's fun to sort of push boundaries and get outside my comfort zone, though, um..."

"Though sometimes you end up having sex on the pool table with a very loud vibrator right before me and his father come home," my mother says, nodding twice. "I completely understand."

"Mom! You can't just say--"

And there they are. Ethan and his dad. Me and my mom are standing in the checkout line at the store now, about to get our clothes rung up, but Ethan and his dad come up to wait with us.

Ethan looks... strange... I don't know how to explain that one. Maybe it's just a side effect of the fact that we're supposed to pretend we don't like each other for his dad's sake. I think that's kind of a weird way to explain it, but I understand why it's necessary. Does it hurt him, though? Ethan?

I never really thought about it. I thought that we'd tell his dad as soon as we could, but before that it would be kind of fun to keep it our secret. Like clandestine lovers, you know? The two of us sneaking away for a moment's reprieve, and better enjoying the time we did have together until we could come out in the open.

I don't know if that's the truth of it or not, though.

"Hey," my stepdad says, smiling to me and my mom. "How's everything?"

"Good," my mom says. "We're just finishing up here."

"Hey, Ethan," I say to him, offering him a small smile.

He shrugs, doesn't smile. "Hey."

"I guess we'll go wait in the car if you're all set," Ethan's dad says. "We should have everything good to go for tomorrow. Just the packing, but I think we'll be able to leave by noon and get to the campsite a few hours before dusk to set up the tents."

"Yeah, it'll be great," Ethan says, though he doesn't sound very into it. "Three tents, one big happy family. Awesome."

There's something off, and now I know it, but I can't ask him about it. I think my mom might realize it, too, but Ethan's dad doesn't seem to notice. Actually... there's something a little off with him, too? Maybe that's just my imagination. I feel like I know Ethan a lot better than his dad, for obvious reasons.

I can ask Ethan when we get home. I hope it's nothing too bad. I... I'm worried? Maybe, sort of, a little...

# 6 - Ethan

WE'RE HOME AND EVERYONE HAS PLANS. My dad's going to work on some last minute business stuff in his office in preparation for us going off grid for awhile. I get it, it's cool, he doesn't want to fuck this trip up with unexpected business junk so he's making sure that it's all taken care of and someone else can handle it while we're going.

Ashley and her mom are going into the living room to sort through their clothes. I really don't get that one. What's with women and their fascination with looking at the stuff they already bought? Didn't they look at it in the store? They were together, too, so it's not like either of them missed anything, but they're sorting through it and checking it out again anyways. Who am I to judge?

Me? What am I doing? Uh... yeah... about that...

"Hey," I say to no one in particular. "I'm going upstairs."

My dad shrugs and says good night. Ashley's mom does, too. It's not that late, but it's late enough that going upstairs is basically saying I probably won't be coming back down. Ashley sort of says good night, but she gives me this weird, confused look.

Yeah, you know what? I'm confused too, Princess. Not sure what to tell you.

I head upstairs, go to my room, close my door, and get undressed. I wasn't exactly planning on going to sleep already, but I just kind of want to lay down. Maybe close my eyes, forget about what happened. It's not that big of a deal, is it? I already knew that my dad didn't agree with me on most things, and this is just another thing we can disagree on.

It just seems big this time, though. Yeah, we've disagreed on my grades before, and I totally get that, but I still passed. I didn't pass with flying colors, and sometimes I barely made it through, but I graduated. I was good enough at football that I got a scholarship to a decent school, so there's that, too. It's not like I'm completely ruining my life here. And so what if I am? It's my life to ruin.

And girls. Yeah, we've argued about that. It's more that he got tired of dealing with them trying to call, call, call. They'd call my cell phone, and when I blocked them, they'd call the house, or sometimes they'd actually come to the house. Is that my fault? Yeah, uh... I guess it is, but I never told them to do any of that stuff.

And so on, and so forth. Oh well. It's all in the past.

This thing with Ashley isn't in the past, though. It's now. It's vibrant and alive and it's happening as we speak, except my dad doesn't approve. Which, yeah, this usually wouldn't bother me, except it's our family, so it's a little bigger than just me now. What happens if my dad disapproves and refuses to let Ashley and I be a couple while we're back home? We can do it anyways, sure, but it just fucks things up. It causes too much tension. It'll ruin shit that I don't want to ruin, and I guess I've never really considered something like that was possible before.

Well, you know what? It is! Surprise!

It's like a birthday present, but the opposite. Pretty much it fucking sucks.

I thought I locked my door when I came into my room, but I guess not, because it's opening right now. There's a pair of eyes peeking through the small crack of the open door, staring into the dark room. I've got those blackout curtains that block out all outside light, so it's dark as fuck in here, but the eyes stare right at me anyways.

"Ethan?" Ashley says, quiet and inquisitive.

"Hey," I say. "What's up?"

"Um... nothing... what are you doing?"

"What's it look like I'm doing?" I ask.

"I don't know. I can't see. Why's it so dark?"

She opens the door more and sneaks in, then closes it behind her. Now we're both in the dark. Ashley has the good sense to lock the door, though. I probably should have locked the door. I don't know if I can deal with her at the moment. I don't even know if I can deal with myself. Weird.

"Are you--Ow!" She fumbles in the dark, trying to get to my bed, but apparently she just crashed into my footboard. The bed shakes and I laugh.

"Are you laughing at me?" she asks. I can picture her brow furrowed, glaring at me.

"Nah, Princess, of course not," I say. "I'm laughing at the other girl crashing around my room in the dark."

"There's no other girl in here!" she says.

"What, there's not?"

"Nope!"

"Oh, huh."

"Don't be mean to me," she says. "Rule number seventeen."

"Well, fuck," I say.

"Well, fuck," she says back.

It sounds so out of place and weird coming from her lips that I laugh.

"Why are you sleeping already?" she asks.

There's something more to the question, and I'm pretty sure I know what it is. Despite my best intentions, my cock twitches in excitement. Yeah... why *am* I sleeping?

It's just... I... nah...

"Listen, Princess," I tell her, trying to figure out how to say this. I don't even fucking want to say it, but I think it's something I should say. "I don't think we should do this."

"Oh," she says, confused. "If you're tired then we can--"

"Nah, it's not that," I say, interrupting her. "I mean, uh... everything? I don't know if we should do what we're doing. Not just tonight, but..."

"Wait, um... Ethan?" she says.

"Yeah?"

"Are you trying to break up with me or something?"

"Look, it's not that I'm trying to break up with you," I say. "Actually, yeah, that's what I was saying, that we should uh... maybe consider it, because..."

I don't fucking know. I don't want to break up with her, but maybe it's for the best? I have no idea what I was thinking before, thinking we could somehow make this work? It's because I don't think about anything. I don't think things through. I figured if she was down with it, it was a good idea, because she's the smart one, right? If it was stupid, I thought she'd realize it before I did, and uh... yeah, after that little heart-to-heart talk with my dad at the sporting goods store, I have finally realized it's stupid, so...

"You can't break up with me," she says. "It's a rule."

"Princess, that's not even a rule. There's no rule saying I can't break up with you."

"I'm making it a rule right now," she says. "Rule number twenty. Ethan Colton, you can't break up with me. So there!"

"What the fuck, that's a shitty rule," I tell her. "Also I was breaking up with you before you even came up with the rule."

"Rules are retroactive," she says.

"The fuck they are! That makes no sense. Most of the rules make no sense at all if they're retro-active."

She finally manages to fumble her way to the side of my bed without crashing into something, and then she does some stuff. I can't see it, but I can hear it, and it sounds like she's stripping down, taking off her clothes. Mostly the zipper on her shorts, but there's a rustle and I think that's her shirt? Fuck if I know, since it's way too dark in here to tell.

You know what, though? Why's she getting naked when I'm breaking up with her? That's a really screwed up response if you ask me. Who does that?

Ashley, I guess. And now she's getting under the blankets with me, too. This girl is weird. Yeah, my stepsister is weird as fuck and I don't know what to do about it. She probably already knows, so there's no point in telling her.

"Why do you want to break up with me?" she asks. "What happened?"

"Are you seriously asking me this?" I ask her. "Who does that?"

"Me," she says. "I do."

"I guess you do."

She cuddles close to me, and I try to be indifferent, but basically as soon as she puts her hand over my chest, I'm done. Also, she's not naked. I can feel her bra brushing against my skin. It's cool, I guess. I've still got my underwear on, too, so whatever. This is probably for the best. I don't think it's possible for two people to break up when they're naked in bed together, but I don't know for sure. Never tried it before. Seems confusing.

"Is it your dad?" she asks.

"Yeah, kind of," I say.

"What happened?"

I wish she'd stop this. Maybe if I just tell her, then we can get this over and done with? I don't want it done. I'm not even being all that serious here, and I'm pretty sure that's why she doesn't believe me, but uh... yeah... we really should consider the consequences of our actions here. How fucked up is it for me to be the one thinking that, though? Who am I and what have I done with Ethan? Wow.

"I was talking with my dad," I say. "I don't know how we got onto this, but we were talking about Jake, and I told my dad that he was a dick, and that if I were dating someone like you I'd never do that. He said that I'd done it before already, and that if he was your father he wouldn't want me dating you, or someone like you, either. So there you go. My dad doesn't know, and when he finds out, he's already told me he disapproves, so what's the point?"

"Well, it doesn't really matter, does it?" she asks.

"Uh, yeah, it kind of matters, Princess. I don't want to be the reason why our family is ruined. You and your mom are good people. I don't want to do that to you."

"It's not like we have to tell him," she says. "Maybe it's good that you found out now, so we can keep it a secret."

"I don't want to keep it a secret," I say.

It's true, too. I guess I never realized it before now, but I don't. I thought we should keep it a secret at first, but that was also when I thought this was just going to be a "with benefits" set up for a week. After the week was up, I fully planned on just cutting ties with her. But, yeah, guess what? The week was up yesterday, and we changed our entire agreement. Rule number one, it's only for a week? Yeah, fuck you, rule number one. Get out of here.

A week and a day isn't all that much better, though, and that's what I'm trying to do here, but...

"I don't, either," Ashley says. "We don't have to keep it a secret forever, though. Maybe just for a little while longer?"

"I get it, Ashley," I say. Real talk here, her real name and everything. "I totally understand where you're coming from, but you think my dad's going to change his mind suddenly? You think we even have a lot of time to handle this? What about that douchebag calling the house every day and threatening to fuck shit up?"

"Oh, yeah," she says. "It's something we have to deal with anyways, though, isn't it?"

Fuck. She's right, isn't she? Even if we break up now, we're going to have to tell my dad eventually. Maybe not?

"Your mom could talk to him," I say. "She could tell Jake to fuck off and that he's stupid as fuck and to leave us alone."

"I guess so," Ashley says. "I just... I don't know what's going to happen when I go back to college, either. I'm scared, Ethan."

She curls up against me more, resting her cheek on my shoulder. She's warm. She's way too warm, warmer than anyone has a right to be, and I really like the way she feels when she's touching me. It's soft and sweet and warm and there's a little bit of sensual sexiness there, too. I mean, fuck, we're both almost completely naked, and if I said that wasn't sexy as fuck, I'd be lying.

Also, I'm kind of hard. By kind of, I mean I'm completely hard. I'm just trying to ignore it, you know? Because, let's be serious here for a moment, it's not exactly the best idea to have an erection when you're trying to convince a girl to break up with you.

Ashley's not just any regular girl, though. She's kind of stubborn. Reminds me of myself sometimes. The thought makes me smile.

"Ethan?" she asks.

"Yeah, what's up, Princess?" I say.

"You're hard."

I am, but how does she... *oh*. Why are you doing this to me, Princess? Ugh.

Sometime between now and uh... awhile ago? Fuck if I know. Anyways, she moved her hand from my chest, down my stomach, to my underwear, which she decided was in the way, so she pulled the front down, and, yeah, she's stroking my cock. *Fuck.*

Seriously. Fuck.

"What are you doing?" I ask her. "You can't do that shit, Princess."

"Nope, I can," she says. "You're my boyfriend."

"Alright, look, I already told you--"

"Can I give you a blowjob?" she asks.

This is the most difficult question of my life. I literally don't know how to answer this. This is not the sort of thing she's supposed to ask me right now.

"It would make me feel better," she says.

*Her?* It would make *her* feel better? What. How does that make sense?

"Oh yeah?" I ask. This is supposed to be more of a question, but do you know how hard it is to think when there's a hand stroking your erection? Try it sometime and get back to me, let me know how that goes. If you don't have a cock, borrow one from someone else.

"Mhm," she murmurs. "Please?"

Holy fuck. Seriously, she doesn't play fair. You know a thesaurus, like a dictionary but for similar words uh... synonyms. Yeah, that's it. Except the opposite, so not synonyms. Fucking... antonyms! That's it. Man, I'm good at this.

Anyways, this is that. Ashley is the antonym of playing fair. The dictionary definition of it.

"Yeah, uh... I mean, go right ahead?" I say, trying to sound casually indifferent. This is hard. Like my cock. Worst analogy ever and I don't even give a fuck. "If you really want to, have a great time."

"Will you have a good time, too?" she asks.

"You're asking me if I'm going to have a good time with you sucking my cock? Is that a real question?"

"Kind of."

"Look, Princess, you do you, and always be yourself. If this is your true calling in life, then have at it. This doesn't change anything, though."

"I will make you change your mind, Ethan Colton," she says, whispering into my ear, sultry as fuck.

"Oh yeah?"

"Yup..."

# 7 - Ashley

CAME UP HERE INTENT ON cheering Ethan up, and, um... well, that's exactly what I'm going to do! I kind of also came up here because I couldn't stop thinking about what we did in the restaurant bathroom earlier. Or the game room before that. Or...

There's a lot of times I can't stop thinking about, and while it's true that a lot of them are the sexy kind of memory, they aren't all that, either. There's more, and there will be even more than that in the future, too. We have a lot of memories ahead of us, don't we?

I just... I don't understand sometimes. I don't understand how we're supposed to do this. If it was just us, I know exactly how we'd do it, and we did that exact thing when our parents were away, but with other people around, everything becomes more and more complicated.

My mom is fine with everything. I think she is, at least. But Ethan's dad isn't? I know they have some issues they've been working through, and I realize maybe it's going to take some time, but how much time? How long do we need to keep this a secret?

I kind of want to run away with him. We could, I think. At least for a little while. We could go on a trip to somewhere entirely different and be alone again, where no one would know us or judge us or say we should or shouldn't do something. They'd just smile and nod and we could talk with them and make friends and have fun and enjoy ourselves.

I fully plan on doing that last one no matter what. In fact, I think I'm about to enjoy myself a lot.

Ethan gets a little, um... excited? I haven't really had a chance to give him a proper blowjob since the first time in the shower, and... it was hot. Sexy. Is that weird? I don't know if that's weird. I kind of want to ask Ethan if that's weird, except I don't think it's weird because he likes doing the same sort of thing to me. It just seems weird because why give him a blowjob or have him eat me out if we can just have sex?

Oh my God, did I just think that? Eat me out? I don't know what I'm becoming. A sex freak, maybe. Good girls definitely can't be sex freaks, but I kind of want to be one with Ethan. I want to be a good girl still, though. I want to do well in school and get good grades and...

And I want to give my stepbrother a blowjob.

No, of course there's no disconnect there. Yes, this is completely regular. Um...

I'm weird. It's easier not to think about it. Especially right now.

I slip beneath the blankets, hiding under them like I'm making myself a night fort and hiding from a monster in the dark. Except I'm pretty sure the monster is in the fort with me...

I move between Ethan's legs. He has his underwear on still, but I don't like that. I need free access here! Without saying anything, I slip my fingers into the waistband of his underwear and tug on them. He lifts up his hips and lets me slide them down his legs. I toss aside this unnecessary piece of clothing, throwing it off the side of the bed.

Mmm... this is going to be fun. I wonder if I can do it like before? With the trick he taught me?

I just want to feel him in my mouth first. I just want to touch him. Greedy and excited, I wrap my fingers around his shaft and stroke him up and down. I hear a muffled groan from above the covers and Ethan squirms under my smooth strokes.

"Fuck, that's good," he says.

If he thinks that's good, well... I waste no time in going even further. While I stroke him up and down slowly, I open my mouth and take the head of his cock between my lips. No precursor, no warning, just a sudden warm wetness around his cock. I keep stroking him while I suck and lick around his smooth cockhead, tasting the curves near his shaft. His hips buck up, almost pushing more of his cock into my mouth, but I react quick and pull back a little.

After a moment, he calms down and lowers himself to the bed. *Ethan? Calm?* We'll see about that...

I bob my head down fast and take half of his cock in my mouth before he realizes my plan. He starts to buck his hips up again, but I planned for this, too. My hands push hard against his thighs, keeping him contained. I know Ethan is stronger than me, and if we were in any other position he could probably overpower me easily, but I have the vantage point here.

This is science and math all combined, and while those aren't exactly my best subjects in school, I still excelled in them. Proper angles, physics, fulcrums... who knew these concepts were useful for giving someone a blowjob? Apparently my good girl skills are multi-purpose, which um... I do not think any of my professors at college would approve of this exact use, but they aren't here so what do I care?

I bob up and down on Ethan's cock fast, forcing heavy sensation through his cock. I hum slightly at the same time, because I read something about that. Vibrations? Well, I like vibrations, so...

My tongue licks and laps at the underside of Ethan's shaft, focusing on the tightness between the head of his cock and his shaft. Oh, yes... that's the frenulum... I'm very good at this, apparently. Anatomy, science, math, and sex, all in one? Um, yes please?

It's kind of fun in a weird way. I mean, it's fun giving Ethan a blowjob in and of itself, but it's exciting in a way that I think is weird to get excited about when I consider the fact that I'm using school ideas to do it better. Who knew good grades would be so useful?

Judging by the way Ethan's thrashing on the bed right now, they're *very* useful, too.

I ease up slightly and move my head back, leaving his cock bereft of my mouth. I take his shaft in one hand and stroke him fast, very fast. Ethan grunts and mumbles incoherently. I think it's incoherent, but to be honest I can barely hear him through the excitement of my own heartbeat pounding in my ears.

Everything seems so much *more* right now. We're in complete darkness, and I can't see a thing, so it's like learning to use all the rest of my senses instead. I can feel the tensing of his thighs and the tightening of his stomach, his cock twitching and throbbing in my hand. I can feel his warmth and the warmth of my breath beneath the blankets. I hear him, both his grunting and his body wrestling with the silken sheets on his bed.

The taste of him lingers on my tongue. It's hard to describe what exactly Ethan tastes like, but his cock is smooth and I like the feeling of it in my mouth. If I'm being honest, I kind of like the feeling of it everywhere. It feels perfect in my hand, in my mouth, pressed against my stomach when we're kissing, and then... it feels very *very* perfect when he's inside me, buried all the way in me, my pussy clenching tight against him, wanting more and more of him.

I can smell him, his heat and his scent. He has a sweet spice to him, like vanilla musk, and at first I thought it was cologne or something, but it's just always there. Ethan has cologne, but he smells amazing without it, too. Who am I to complain about something like that?

I feel him throbbing even more in my hand, growing more excited by the moment. I pick up the pace, stroking him faster and faster, even faster still.

"Holy fuck, Princess, what are you doing to me?" he says with a grunt.

"Do you want me to stop?" I call out from beneath the covers.

I slow down a little and grin. I want to see what he'll do and what he'll say.

"Don't stop," he says, frantic. "Please don't fucking stop. Holy shit, this feels so fucking good, you don't even know."

He did say please, didn't he? I like that he's a bad boy with manners.

I take him into my mouth again. I can taste more of him now, the slick arousal of his precum lubricating the head of his cock. I mix it with the wetness of my mouth and trail it along his cock with my tongue, enjoying the taste. It's a little sweet and a little something more, and I completely adore it. I'm insatiable, I want more, I *must* have it.

Oh, Ethan, do you want to give it to me, too? I grin imagining his answer.

His thighs tense even more, squeezing against me. I stroke him while I lick and suck on the head of his cock. I want to try more now, but I realize this isn't exactly the best position. The shower was easier to take all of him into my mouth, because of how we were positioned at the time, but um... I can try, right?

I make a fist with my left hand and squeeze my thumb in it. I lower myself as far as I can onto Ethan's cock, taking as much of him as possible in my mouth. I feel him pressing against the back of my throat, and I try to take more of him, but I was right and we just aren't in a very good position for it. Still, I have a lot of him in my mouth. I think I like it. I think I like it a lot.

I ease back up and then go back down, taking as much of him as I can again. My tongue licks around his shaft, teasing at his pulsing veins. He's so very very close, I can tell, and I want to make him even closer, more than close.

I take my free hand and the next time I push down as far as I can onto his cock, I cup his balls lightly in my palm and then massage and roll them in my fingers. They tighten and tense in my hands, just like his thighs next to me. His cock twitches and throbs even more in my mouth.

Mmm... yes. Please, Ethan? I beg him with my mouth, but without words. I coax him with my tongue and my lips and my hand.

"Holy fuck I'm--"

He doesn't have a chance to say more before his words become a wild mess of contradiction. I have no idea what he's saying, but to be honest I'm barely even listening. I'm preparing. I am ready! *Yesss...*

Ethan explodes, giving into his baser needs. His body tightens, all of his muscles tense and restricted, and then all of a sudden I feel it. My lips are wrapped around the head of his cock as he starts to cum, but I push myself down his shaft, taking as much of him in as I can. I feel the first splash of him against the roof of my mouth. As I tease and massage his balls, I feel another jet of cum roll across my tongue, and then one more splashing against the inside of my cheek. I hold his orgasm in my mouth, continuing to suck and bob up and down on his cock.

He's done. He's not cumming anymore, but I keep going. I go more, refusing to stop, waiting for...

Ethan starts to squirm and laugh and he tries to grab me but I'm still under the covers. I keep going, knowing full well he's too sensitive right now. It's fun, though. I like it a lot and I want to make him feel me and remember everything. Finally he realizes the only way to stop me is to pull the blankets off completely, so in one smooth sweep he does exactly that.

I was warm and hidden beneath the blankets but now I'm exposed to the cool air of his room. He sneaks away from me, managing to pull me out from between his legs, and then he lifts me up and onto his chest. He tries to kiss me, but I turn my head away at the last minute so he kisses my cheek instead.

Careful, I open my mouth and say, "I still haf your cum in my mouf."

"Oh yeah?" he asks. I can feel his smirk against my cheek as he kisses me. "What are you going to do with that?"

I answer him by doing it. I lick my lips, and I swallow, and then I lick my lips again. Quick, before he can stop me, I turn back and I kiss him. He seems surprised at first, but then he kisses me back. Our tongues fight with one another for dominance, but I'm pretty sure Ethan's tongue wins. His hands reach behind me and squeeze my butt hard, pulling me tight against him.

"You swallowed, huh?" he asks.

"Mhm," I murmur. "You taste good."

"Do you know how fucking hard you make me, Princess?" he asks, laughing.

"I think I have a pretty good idea..." I say, trailing off.

I can still feel him, his erection between my legs. It's not as hard as it was when I had him in my mouth, but it's still plenty hard. The head of his cock pokes and prods at my sex, but I've still got my panties on.

Apparently Ethan doesn't like that, because...

Before I realize it, he sneaks past my defenses, pulls my panties to the side, and then pulls me down onto his cock. I fall easily, becoming impaled on his cock even easier. Really, it's the easiest thing in the world. It's basically perfect. It's...

I let out a gasp, not expecting this, but really really enjoying it. He's not as hard as before, and I don't know if he's going to stay hard for long, but I want to revel in the feeling of him inside me while I still can.

"What... what are you doing?" I ask him.

"I fucking love being inside you," he says. "Seriously, I can't get enough of it."

"I just gave you a blowjob," I remind him, grinning and kissing him quick.

"Yeah, so?"

"You sure do like sex a lot," I say to him.

"Yeah, so?"

I lift my hips up a little and then move back down. Mmm... this is nice. I wiggle my hips when he's all the way inside me and settle down even more. I feel Ethan twitch and throb.

"I want to make love to you," I tell him.

"This feels really nice," he says. "Perfect as fuck, Princess, don't get me wrong. I'm just going to need a little time here."

"How much time?" I ask.

"Are you seriously asking me that?" he asks, laughing. "Fuck... I don't know. A couple minutes?"

"Alright!" I say. I have an idea. I think it's a good one.

# 8 - Ethan

Fuck if I know what she's doing, but Ashley reaches to the side, bringing my cock with her. It bends to accommodate her movement, and I almost slip out of her, but whatever she was reaching for, she got it, so uh... yeah, we're back in business here. She slides up and down my cock a couple times before moving down to whisper in my ear.

"I brought a toy," she says.

Whoa, wait. Holy fuck. Does that mean what I think it does? Wait, no, really, what's that mean? I'm not even sure. I mean, I'm pretty sure I'm going to love it whatever it means, but I'm not following her logic here.

"So..." she says, sultry and sweet. "While I'm waiting for you, I think I'm going to play."

"Oh yeah?" I ask her.

"Do you want to see?" she asks.

Do you know how fast it takes to turn on a light? Bedside lamp, within arm's reach, about the same distance that Ashley just reached. Yeah, I don't even know how long, but maybe faster than the speed of light. Or the speed of sound. Or none of those. It's pretty fucking fast, though. My hand shoots out and I flick the switch on the lamp on my bedside table faster than I can think.

She's there, in all her perfect fucking beautiful gorgeous glory, sitting on my cock. It's sexy as fuck and cute at the same time, which is hard to explain. She's still got her bra and panties on, and they're cute and white, almost like she's some pure angel, except uh... yeah, Little Miss Perfect Angel over here just gave me the most amazing blowjob ever.

Seriously, where did she learn these skills? Pretty sure I don't even care, but I'm impressed either way.

Without saying a word, she turns on her toy. It's small and fits easily in the palm of her hand, but it's thick, like, uh... alright, don't take this the wrong way here, but it's about as thick around as my cock, which is to say it's got some good girth to it. When she turns it on, it starts to buzz and vibrate. Nothing crazy, not like the insane vibrator we used before, but it's got some decent noise to it.

She tugs at the front of her panties, pulling them forward, then slips the toy into them, pressing it against her clit. The feeling is instant and sharp, and the craziest part is I can feel it, too.

I feel her clench around my cock as soon as she presses the toy against her clit, and then I can feel the heavy vibrations of it pulsing through my cock. She must feel it more, but the fact that I can feel it, too...

What the fuck did I tell her before? I can't even remember. Whatever it was, it was a lie. I didn't mean to lie, and yeah, I thought it would take me a couple minutes to get ready for her again. But, nah, I'm good to go. Hard as fuck, ready and willing.

I would. I really fucking would. I would slam this girl onto my bed and fuck her hard or make love to her for hours or whatever she wants, but I kind of want to see how this plays out. Also, it's just sexy as fuck, and it feels amazing for me, too. Weird? I don't even care.

My cock thickens and throbs inside her while the vibrations from her toy course through us, and her pussy clenches against me. Ashley lifts up a little, then down, riding me slowly. She holds the toy against her clit and closes her eyes, biting her bottom lip. Up again, down, slow, concentrating, lost in thought.

"You're so fucking hot, Princess," I tell her, whispering, my voice husky. "This is the sexiest thing I've ever done, no joke."

Her eyes open, wide, and she looks at me, surprised. "Really?" she asks, her voice timid.

I give her a huge grin and nod. "Yeah. I wouldn't lie to you," I tell her.

"I... Ethan, can I cum? Like this?"

"You're asking me?" I ask, laughing. "What did I tell you before, baby girl? You do you. Always be yourself and follow your dreams."

She rolls her eyes at me and then slaps at my chest. Oh yeah? You want to play that game?

I buck my hips up, pushing hard into her. Her eyes roll into the back of her head and she lets out a quick gasp. Sexy as fuck, that's what that is. She closes her eyes after that, concentrating again, pressing the toy against her clit and moving it a little, side to side.

I watch her, just really watch her. Usually I'm caught up in the moment, and there's a lot going on, but this is kind of relaxing in a weird way. We're not really moving, just enjoying each other. I'm really really fucking enjoying her, but still.

Her stomach tightens a little. I push up into her again, slow and steady, and her stomach tightens even more. She hitches her breath when I shift back down, and then opens her mouth to let out a lusty sigh when I lift up again, her stomach tight once more. I reach out and rest my hand on her hip, my thumb tracing a line against the muscles in her stomach that tighten whenever I roll my hips up and push into her.

She rolls her hips against me, too. It's not exactly thrusting or pushing, but just a kind of massage. Yeah, I like that idea of that. Cock and pussy massage? Sounds amazing to me. Definitely relevant as fuck to my interests.

The vibrations are still there. The clutching of her inner walls as she gives in to pleasure, too. I can feel it more deeply, probably because I'm focusing on it. There's not a lot of movement right now. It reminds me of when I'm about to cum, when I thrust deep inside of her, and when she cums at the same time, except neither of us are cumming right now. It's just a constant throb, pulse, vibration, over and over, our hips rolling, our bodies grinding together.

I'm pretty fucking sure this is amazing. Pretty fucking sure...

"Ethan, I..." she says, stopping with a gasp.

"Let go, Princess," I say to her. "Cum for me, alright?"

She nods, eyes closed, her bottom lip tucked between her teeth. "Mhm..."

She presses something on her toy and the buzzing intensifies. Holy fuck, it has more settings? The vibrations intensify, and I seriously wasn't expecting this. I am not prepared for this. I...

Seriously, fuck, this feels amazing.

What I was planning on doing once she finished up was, uh... well, tossing her onto the bed and having my way with her. Notice I said I was planning on doing this. I don't know what I'm planning on doing now. I can't really think about it. Just give me a second, will you?

I close my eyes to try and think, because this is getting real really fast, and then uh...

Wow. Fuck. Wow...

Wow. For real, wow.

There's another setting, apparently. And another. What the fuck kind of toy is this? Apparently Ashley does her homework in more ways than one, and she takes sex toy buying seriously. Who knew?

I'm done. I did not plan for this. I don't think I ever could have planned for this. Seriously, though, it's uh... it's a lot. I don't want to say too much, but...

My cock is practically alive inside her, buzzing with vibrations and sensations I don't think I've ever felt before. And she's grinding against me, hips swaying back and forth, side to side. Her body squeezes against mine, inside and out. Her pussy presses hard against my cock while the vibrations crash through me.

I feel her cumming. I hear it, too. I can't see it, because my eyes are closed, but I don't even need to see this to know it's a thing of beauty and it's seriously fucking amazing. I grab both her hips in my hands and hold her hard against my cock while she cums and lets out little whimpered gasps of pleasure.

I can do this. I can hold back. I can stick to my plans and...

Nah. Way to go, Ashley. Way to completely ruin this.

Way to make it fucking amazing as fuck... seriously, fuck.

*More, more, more.* In rapid succession, she brings the toy up to full power, and there's some serious vibrations going on. Combined with her orgasm and the fact that she's gripping my cock hard, uh...

I'm done. It's over. I start to cum, too, filling her. She opens her mouth wide as if to say something, but no sounds come out. She clenches and grips against my cock even harder when I start to cum, though.

"Oh... Ethan... Yesss..." she hisses, ecstatic. "Please, I want you inside me. All of you. Please?"

Since she asked so nicely...

Yeah, who am I kidding? I couldn't even stop if I tried.

The crazy thing is it just keeps... going? This is not a normal orgasm. I don't even know how to explain this. I'm pretty fucking sure it's got something to do with the magic in her hands. That's not a sex toy, it's wizardry or something. Ashley Banks is a sex witch, plain and simple.

My orgasm refuses to stop, though I don't think I'm cumming anymore. Fuck if I know what I'm doing. I'm just along for the ride, I guess. Her body trembles and clenches against me and the vibrations keep going and going, thrumming through my cock, keeping me on high alert.

This is bad. It's so bad it's good. This is like before when she kept sucking my cock even after I came in her mouth, and, man, it's sensitive as fuck. It feels amazing, but it's just hard to handle.

And now? This is that but I'm pretty sure it's ten times worse. Can you die of an ecstasy overload? I never would have thought so before, but I think I might change my mind.

Ashley seems to be enjoying herself, too. Her stomach is tight, and inside her I can feel one constant clench. Her fingers turn white pressing the toy against her clit, that's how hard and into it she is, and then she starts to laugh, manic.

Oh no. *Fuck*. She's broken, isn't she? I start to laugh, too, because it's kind of funny but it's not supposed to be funny.

This is really loud, isn't it? What if our parents hear? She locked the door, though, so uh... I don't know, I'll make something up.

She fumbles with the toy pressed against her clit until she finally manages to turn it off, then she pulls it out from the front of her panties and collapses on top of me. Her cheeks are warm and red and her hair is messy and a little wet, probably from sweating. Yeah, this is exercise right here. Great workout, Ashley. Good job, nice lifts.

I slide out of her and roll her to the side, holding her against my body. She sidles close and wraps her arm around me, cuddling.

"Hey, Princess," I say to her.

"Hi, Ethan," she says, eyes closed, smiling.

"What the fuck was that?" I ask.

"Amazing," she says, wistful. "It was amazing."

"Yeah... yeah, it was."

"You came inside me," she says, giggling. "Did it feel good?"

"Good?" I say. "Fuck, I don't even know what good means anymore. That was weird and intense and holy fuck all at once."

"Does this mean you're not going to break up with me?" she asks, grinning and kissing my cheek.

"Yeah, I mean, let's be real, I wasn't going to break up with you before. Also, we've got rules to follow here. Rule number twenty, right?"

"Yup!" she says, giddy. "No breaking up with me!"

"Good!" I say, kissing her fast. "Because I don't want to!"

"But I can break up with you," she adds. "Nyah!"

"What the fuck, did you just nyah at me? Who does that?"

"Me," she says. "I do it. I just did it."

"Yeah, I guess you did," I say, laughing. Quick, I reach over and turn the light off, covering us in darkness again. Light is too much, it's too complicated and confusing right now. I just want to focus on Ashley, I only want to think about her and how she feels in my arms.

"I love you," she says, kissing my cheek.

"I love you, too," I say. "But I've got bad news for you."

"What?" she asks.

"You can't break up with me, either. There's rules for that. Uh... the one where we both have to follow all the rules. They apply to each of us together. Right?"

"Hm... I don't know if I remember that one..." she says. The tone of her voice is a dead giveaway that she definitely knows what I'm talking about. "Which rule was that?"

"Fuck if I know," I say. "You're the one who knows all the numbers."

"If you can't remember it then I don't think that was one of them," she says, defiant.

"Look, Princess. I remember rule number eleven, alright? That's an important one. You can't expect me to remember the rest."

"I do like rule number eleven," she says. "We still haven't, you know? You said we could try to do that all day one time, and you still haven't."

"Listen, I'm not going to spend all day devouring your perfect fucking pussy if I've got to worry about you breaking up with me, too."

"Oh no..." she says, mock fear running through her voice.

"Yeah," I say. "Yeah, you understand now. This is serious business."

"I see..."

"So what we need to do is you need to tell me what rule is the one where all the rules apply to both of us."

"Do you think we need to write them down?" she asks. "We have twenty now. Who knows how high it'll go?"

"Fuck... yeah, I think we might need to do that."

"It's thirteen," she says. "That's the one. So if you can't break up with me, I can't break up with you, either."

"Good," I say. "Don't even try it, Princess. I'm watching you."

"Good!" she says. Then she licks my cheek. "I'm licking you."

"You're crazy," I say, laughing.

She licks me again. Oh, you want to play games here, Princess? I reach for her side and start to tickle her. She laughs and I kiss the tip of her nose. She laughs more, trying to squirm away from me, but I hold her tight.

"Ethan... Ethan!" she gasps. "St-stop, our parents will hear us, they'll..."

I stop. Not because I believe her, though. I stop because I kind of just want to cuddle the fuck out of her right now.

She comes into my arms when I pull her close and she rests her head on my shoulder. Then she licks me.

Wow. Really? Wow.

# 9 - *Ashley*

ETHAN AND I LAY IN BED TOGETHER, cuddling, neither of us speaking. I don't think he's sleeping, though, and I can't sleep, either. I close my eyes and try to block out the worried thoughts in my head, but they don't seem to go away.

What are we going to do? It was easy to ignore Jake when our parents were gone. All we did was mute the call and delete any voicemail messages that he left. Yes, it was frustrating and annoying, but after a couple days it was kind of like an inside joke between us.

Now, though...

"Hey," Ethan says. "You sleeping or what?"

"What kind of question is that?" I ask him, laughing. "If I were sleeping I wouldn't be able to answer you."

"Nah," he says, grinning and kissing me quick. "Maybe you'd talk in your sleep. I don't know."

"Maybe," I say, considering it. "I'm not sure if I'd answer you truthfully if I was asleep, though. I might lie about being asleep."

Ethan sighs and shakes his head. "Yeah, maybe. It might be easier to talk to you in your sleep, too, though."

I stiffen, unsure what he means by that.

"What's that mean?" I ask him. "Is it hard to talk to me when I'm awake?"

"Nah, that's not it," he says. "It's just... fuck, I don't know. My dad and everything. I'm not sure what to do."

Oh. I take a deep breath, trying to think of what to say. "Um... well, we don't have to do anything right away," I tell him. "We can just wait."

"Yeah, but how long?" he asks. "What do we do if that douche ex-boyfriend of yours keeps calling the house, too?"

"It won't matter for long," I remind him. "We're going camping tomorrow, remember?"

"Oh," Ethan says. "Yeah, that's true."

"So we can keep it a secret from him easily while we're gone, and then when we get back we can figure out what to do. I know my mom will help. Maybe she can just answer the phone one time when Jake calls and deal with him then."

"What about after, though?" Ethan asks.

"Huh? What do you mean?"

"Listen, Princess," Ethan says, serious. "This is going to be hard. I know it's fun and all, and I have a great time with you, but this is still kind of fucked up and it's going to be hard. You think just because your mom tells that prick to leave you alone that he's going to do it? Yeah, maybe for the summer it'll work, but what happens when you go back to school?"

"I..." I hesitate, because I didn't want to talk about this so soon. "Ethan, I'm not sure, because it's going to be hard for a lot of reasons."

"Yeah," he says. Then he surprises me by adding, "You think we can make it work?"

"What's that supposed to mean?" I ask him.

"Going to be honest with you here, Princess," he says. "I've never put a lot of time into thinking about how to make a relationship work. I don't do that. I think about how to end them, how to cut girls off, and I try not to be a dick about it, but uh... well, fuck, you know how that used to go."

"Have you thought about how to end it with me?" I ask him.

He takes awhile to answer. "Yeah," he says. "Before, though. Before any of this got real and serious, when it was still just something for the week. I just didn't want to fuck any of this up. I don't know. Are you mad?"

"What do you mean by *before*," I ask him. "How long before?"

"Does it matter? It's an asshole thing to think about any way you cut it, Ashley. I get it, I really do. I'm pretty fucking bad at relationships."

"It matters," I tell him. "Please?"

He waits a few seconds, then says, "Right at the start. Like, seriously, right after you came into the shower with me and I shaved you, and we had some fun. I just didn't want to hurt you. I get what people say about me and the reputation I have, Princess, but I don't want to hurt anyone, you know?"

"You're weird," I tell him, trying not to smile. This is supposed to be serious, but for some reason he always makes me smile. I think he's actually always made me smile, though I know there's some things I should exactly be smiling about.

"I just told you I was thinking about how to end things with you and you tell me I'm weird?" he says. "I think you're the weird one here."

"I just wanted to make sure it wasn't after..."

"After what?" he asks.

"I don't know," I say. "After. Just after."

He shrugs and pulls me close. "Nah, not after. If I'm being brutally fucking honest right now, I'm pretty sure later that same day I was thinking how fucked up it was that I didn't want it to end in a week."

"What? Really?"

"Yeah," he says, smiling. "Well, maybe it was the next morning. Maybe it was in my dreams or something. Fuck if I know."

"How long have you loved me?" I ask him. "I don't know if I'm supposed to ask you that."

"How long have you loved me?" he asks.

"You can't ask me the same thing I just asked you," I say. "That's kind of cheating, don't you think?"

"Nah," he says. "I want to know the answer, too."

"If I tell you first, you'll just say the same thing, though," I whine, playful.

"You think I'd lie to you?" he asks, smirking. "If I tell you first, you could do the same thing."

"Nope! I won't!"

"Yeah, yeah, sure..."

"Do you have a pen and paper?" I ask.

"Huh? Uh... yeah, in my bedside table, probably."

I roll away from him despite him trying to playfully pull me back. I slap at his hands and free myself from his cuddles and slip away to the side of the bed. I flick on the light switch to his lamp and then rummage around through the drawer in his bedside table. I grin and snatch up one of his condoms in there, then throw it at him.

"I better not catch you using these ever again," I tell him while still searching.

"You just going to stay on the pill forever or something?" he asks. "I'm not going to use them with anyone else if that's what you mean."

"I was just teasing you!" I say. I finally find a pen and a pad of paper and take them from the drawer, then return to bed with them. "I'm not going to take birth control forever, either."

"Uh, then we're going to need condoms," he says. "Pretty fucking sure that's how that works, Princess."

"You're so dumb," I say. "How am I going to get pregnant if I'm on birth control?"

"Uh..."

*Uh?* What's that for? I thought it made perfect sense, definitely logical, and um... oh no. Oh my God, did I just um... yes, I said that, didn't I? I didn't mean, er...

"I didn't mean with you!" I say, quick. "That's not what I meant."

"Wait a fucking second here," he says, half angry, half laughing. "If not with me, with who?"

"I didn't mean to say it like that, I mean. I'm going to be on birth control for a long time, Ethan. Maybe twenty years. I don't know."

"Fuck, twenty years? That's a long time?"

"Ten years?" I offer.

"Seems a little better," he says.

I rip off a piece of paper from the pad and hand it to him. "Five years?" I say.

He gives me a weird look, but doesn't say anything.

I wonder how far I can go with this. I kind of just want to tease him a little more. "Three years? Maybe just a year. Six months? A month? A week... I could just stop tomorrow, I guess."

He stares at me, eyes narrowed, one eyebrow raised. "Freak," he says. "I'm keeping these condoms."

"Good!" I say, sticking my tongue out at him. "Really, though, I'm not going to stop taking my birth control for awhile. I don't know how long. I do want to have a baby some day, though."

"Yeah..." he says. "Me, too, just uh..."

"What?"

"We've been dating for almost a week here," he says.

"You're dumb," I say, laughing. "We're not talking about having babies right now, Ethan."

"Holy fucking shit," he says, hiding his laugh, feigning shocked surprise. "Babies? More than one? What the fuck is going on here?"

"Maybe two or three," I say, teasing him. "Who really knows?"

"I'm done," he says, shaking his head. "I can't do this anymore."

"I don't want to have babies now," I say. "Or any time too soon, either. I want to finish college and I want to find what I love to do and put all of my effort into it, and I want to find someone to share that with, too. When he and I are ready, then we can have a serious conversation about babies, though."

"So..." Ethan says, trailing off. "You're not going to include me in this conversation?"

He's giving me this grin. It's a horrible bad boy grin and he's teasing me and I have half a mind to...

I don't know. To love him forever? Is that normal? I kind of want it to be normal, and even if it's not normal I kind of want to do it anyways.

"Maybe," I say, holding onto the word as long as I can. "Maybe we can both finish college together, and we can find something to put all of our effort into together, and we won't have to find someone to share that with because we already have each other. And when we're ready we can have a serious conversation about babies..."

"Yeah," Ethan says. "That could be fun. You know what I like about babies?"

Wait, has he thought about this before? "Um... what?"

He rolls on top of me, spreading my legs easily with his knee, and then he presses himself hard against me. He's got no underwear on still, but I'm still wearing my bra and panties. Ethan slips his hand beneath my underwear and slides his fingers up and down my sex. I gasp, not expecting this, but... I could get used to it. I think I'm already used to it after just a few seconds. His lips touch against mine, kissing me softly, but with a promise of more.

I feel something between my legs, almost inside of me. Oh my God, is that him? Um... yes, his erection. He's hard. Again. Already. I don't even know how, because he already came twice tonight, but apparently that is not Ethan Colton's limit.

"The thing I love about babies," he says, whispering into my ear. "Is the practice before the real event."

He thrusts hard into me, filling me, and I let out a quick gasp. "Ohhhh..."

And... um... then he's done? He pulls out of me and rolls back to his side of the bed, hiding himself beneath the blankets. I scurry under them, too, because I'm getting a little cold, but... I reach between his legs to feel him, and, yes, he's definitely still erect. And his cock is covered in my arousal, which is oddly exciting to me. I kind of want him to be even more covered in my arousal, which I think I know exactly how to do...

"That was my one tease," he says. "I just wanted to get it out of the way now."

"Um...?"

"You know? Rule number nineteen? I can tease you once, and you can tease me once, but after that it's the real deal. So there you go. That was me teasing you."

"Are you being serious right now?" I ask him. "I think that wasn't teasing at all. You should just do it again, but don't stop this time."

"Oh yeah?"

"I think so!"

"See, that's why it's the perfect tease," he says, a smug grin on his face.

"I think," I say, mumbling, "I hate you."

"Hey, you've still got your tease left," he says. "It's not like I cheated with the rules or anything. Anyways, what's with the paper and pen?"

Oh... well, I don't really want to talk about the paper and pen right now. I want to talk about something else that starts with "pen" and ends with "is" and um... it's Ethan's. Penis. That sounded much wittier in my head, except it still sounds witty in my head and I start to giggle uncontrollably.

Then he starts tickling me. Oh no! Eeeek...

"Stop!" I say, smacking his hands away. "Ethan, that's teasing and you already teased me, you can't do it again!"

"Fuck," he says, stopping. Then he thinks about it for a second. "Wait a fucking second... how is tickling you teasing you? Pretty sure it's not."

"No, it is," I say quick before he changes his mind. "Here, um... what did you even do with your piece of paper? You're supposed to hold onto it."

He looks around, then finds it discarded on the floor. "Found it."

I scribble something on my own piece of paper, then hand him the pen.

"Here," I say. "Write down when you fell in love with me. The first time you thought about it, even just a little bit."

"Are you serious?" he says.

"Yup! I wrote it down, and you write it down, then we read what we wrote and we'll know it's true because we wrote it down. Neither of us can cheat that way."

He looks at me, skeptical, but then he shrugs and takes pen to paper and writes something down.

"Alright, what did you write?" I say.

"What did you write?" he asks.

"I asked you first, and, anyways, it's not like I can lie, because I already wrote it down."

"I guess," he says, giving me a look. "Whatever. Fine."

I wait. He doesn't say anything. I wait some more. He still doesn't say anything. I nudge him with my elbow, and finally he says something.

"Second grade," he says. "You happy now?"

"What? Are you serious? Let me see the paper!"

He shows me the paper, and, clear as day, there it is: 2nd grade. It's kind of scribbled and rough, but it's unmistakeable. I stare at it, trying to see if maybe the two could be something else, except that doesn't work because of the "-nd" that follows, and there's no other numbers that would work with that.

"Alright, I told you," he says. "Now you tell me."

"Um..."

"What?" he asks, giving me another look.

"Second grade, too," I say, slowly.

"Seriously?" he asks, surprised but grinning.

"Mhm, yup. Of course," I say.

He... why is he looking at me like that? Stop it! "Let me see your paper, Princess," he says.

"You don't believe me?" I say, trying to sound upset. "I thought you loved me, Ethan?"

He's having none of it. He playfully wrestles me to the bed and steals the paper away from me after I laugh and try to stop him from tickling me.

I am done, though. He has stolen my paper.

*Fuck.* I don't like swearing, but this is a very "fuck" kind of situation and I don't like that, either.

"You're a huge liar," he says, staring at the words I wrote. "Wow, fifth grade? That's a bunch of bullshit."

"It's because I didn't want you to feel bad," I say, sticking out my tongue at him. "That's why I wrote that. I thought you would write something like when we first kissed at that party when we were fifteen so I didn't want you to feel bad, but really it was second grade, too."

"Yeah," he says, grinning. "I remember that kiss. That was nice."

"Also you're a huge jerk and you kissed four other girls that night," I remind him.

"Listen, Princess, if you would have just fucking told me you wanted to kiss me before I invited everyone over, I wouldn't have invited anyone over and we could have spent the entire night kissing. Don't go blaming this on me."

"You're lying," I tell him. Is he lying? Um...

"Here's the truth," he says. "I don't know if I fell in love with you in second grade, but I really liked you a lot. I always kept an eye out when you were around, and I was hoping you'd find a nice guy to date, but I was scared, too, because if I saw you with some guy, I'm pretty sure I would have gotten jealous as fuck. That night before the party, I told all the guys you were off limits and if they tried to screw around with you, I'd send them the fuck home in a body bag. Get it?"

Oh... "So you did lie," I say, trying to hide the blush creeping into my cheeks. "You didn't fall in love with me in second grade."

"Maybe," he says. "Fuck if I know. I just wish we'd gotten together sooner, but maybe I needed to learn how to appreciate someone or else I would have fucked it up. I just know that I've wanted to appreciate you for a long time."

I don't know what to say, but I need to answer him, so I do, with my lips but no words. I fling myself onto him, twining my fingers in his hair, kissing him. Ethan puts his hands on my hips and pulls me closer to him. I can feel him between my legs, hard, but this isn't about that right now. For all I know it'll be about that in a couple of seconds, but just not right now.

"I don't want to lose you, Ashley," Ethan says, smiling and kissing me. "I know this seems fucked up, but my dad made it pretty clear what he thinks about this, though. Can we keep it a secret from him for awhile? I'll try to get on his good side or something, break it to him then, but I think I'm going to need a little time here."

"Can we sneak away on the camping trip, though?" I ask.

"Oh yeah? What do you want to sneak away for?" he asks me with a grin.

"To, um... talk..."

"That's it?"

"And maybe kiss..."

"Anything else?"

"And have sex..."

"I bet I can think of a few places we can sneak away to for all those things," he says, smirking and winking at me. "It'll work."

I lay back down, and reach over to turn the light off. Ethan pulls me into his arms as soon as I do, and we cuddle together, kissing every so often in the dark. I like how warm he is when I'm holding him, and how comfortable I feel laying against him. It's nice. I've never had anything like this before, never had anyone like him before, and...

I don't think he's had anything like this or anyone like me, either. I know he hasn't. I've known him for so long, and yet it kind of feels like I'm only just beginning to know him, too. It's fun, like a discovery or an adventure.

"I love you, Princess," Ethan says, whispering into my ear.

"I love you, too," I tell him, whispering back.

Even if we have to keep our relationship a secret from his dad, I think this camping trip will be fun. It's like a camping trip with secret benefits, right?

# A NOTE FROM MIA

THINGS ARE PICKING UP AND GETTING EXCITING! I really loved writing this episode for season two and I hope you loved reading it just as much. There's some fun things going on and I love watching Ethan and Ashley playing and talking and having fun with each other. I think the sexy stuff is really fun, too, haha.

This opens up more of what season two is going to be about, so I just wanted to talk about that for a second. While Ashley's mom was accepting of their relationship because I think she's a little more understanding of it all, it would appear that Ethan's dad isn't quite of the same mindset. There's some history behind that, and him and Ethan don't have the same sort of relationship as Ashley and her mom have, either. Like Ethan's dad said at one point, it's kind of a work in progress for the two of them.

This is going to be hard, though! Sneaking around, and um... well, on the camping trip they're all going to be a lot closer together than they are now. With Ethan's dad and Ashley's mom sleeping downstairs, Ethan and Ashley can sneak around a lot easier upstairs, but when they're all right next to each other in thin tents while camping... this is going to be interesting...

I hope you're enjoying the second season so far! The camping trip is coming next and there's going to be a lot going on there. Some of it will be exciting and steamy, some will be a little silly and funny, and there's bound to be tension and drama, too.

If you liked this episode, I'd love if you rated and reviewed it! I really appreciate it and it's nice to see what everyone thinks. I hope you liked it a lot!

Don't forget to sign up for my VIP readers list if you haven't, too. You'll get first notice on when my next book is released, so you'll never miss a thing. More Ethan and Ashley will be coming soon, don't worry!

Bye for now!

~MIA

# ABOUT THE AUTHOR

Mia likes to have fun in all aspects of her life. Whether she's out enjoying the beautiful weather or spending time at home reading a book, a smile is never far from her face. She's prone to randomly laughing at nothing in particular except for whatever idea amuses her at any given moment.

Sometimes you just need to enjoy life, right?

She loves to read, dance, and explore outdoors. Chamomile tea and bubble baths are two of her favorite things. Flowers are especially nice, and she could get lost in a garden if it's big enough and no one's around to remind her that there are other things to do.

She lives in New Hampshire, where the weather is beautiful and the autumn colors are amazing.

Made in the USA
San Bernardino, CA
25 March 2017